*The Hoodlum Game*

# THE

# HOODLUM

# GAME

*David R. Stookey*

# TABLE OF CONTENTS

# Chapter 1 - A Chance Discovery

Eddie Ponzino felt a warm blast of sunshine as he stepped through the door to his back yard. His mom had slept in, so he took care not to slam the door behind him. The cloudless sky above the trees promised an exciting day.

Eddie's best friend and neighbor, Mike Ashland, had agreed to go fishing with him this morning. Thanks to Mike's soccer schedule, Eddie had to fish alone these past several weekends. He welcomed the opportunity to catch up on the latest school gossip.

To his right, an enormous back yard featured a park-like setting of flower gardens, footpaths and even a working fountain.

Old Lady Lauffer lived there, and employed a small army of gardeners to maintain the property. Like the Ashlands' yard to his left, the lawn and landscaping looked picture perfect.

In sharp contrast, the "Ponzino Estate," as his mother called their own property, consisted of a featureless rectangle of crabgrass and burnt patches of lawn. A rusting metal shed stood against the back wall of the house.

Eddie collected his well-seasoned spinning rod and tackle box from the shed. He checked his watch and glanced at his neighbor's back door. Great timing! He could see Mike waving goodbye to someone inside as he backed out onto the deck. Eddie started over to meet him halfway, then stopped dead in his tracks. Mike's bikini clad sister had stepped through the door right behind him. Juggling a small cooler, cell phone, portable speaker, towel and sunglasses, she struggled with the door. Mike closed it for her, but smirked and rolled his eyes at Eddie. Cindy clearly planned to spend the day tanning by the pool and jabbering with her friends on the phone.

"Hey, Cindy!" Eddie said, trying to sound casual while not staring at her. About a year ago, he'd noticed that Cindy had grown from Mike's annoying little sister into quite a cutie. Though only two years behind the boys in school, she used to seem so much younger. Almost overnight she had developed a slender golden-tanned figure, shoulder length blonde hair, a stunning smile and the bluest eyes Eddie had ever seen. He adored her, but sensed she was way out of his league.

Cindy either didn't hear him or didn't care. She thwacked her way down the deck stairs to the pool in her flip-flops, never looking back. Eddie considered yelling to her again, but didn't want to look desperate. Over the years, he and Cindy had always tolerated each other with polite greetings. He had not yet mustered the nerve to push beyond that. He couldn't bear the thought of her rejecting him outright, or maybe even laughing at him. On top of that, he didn't know how Mike would react.

"Man, great day for fishing, or what?" Mike grinned from ear to ear.

Eddie tried to recall if he had ever seen Mike without his beaming smile. Mike hefted his huge tackle box and fancy rod case from the storage box under their deck and jogged across the yard to join Eddie.

"Yeah! Forecast said clouds and light rain, but all I can see is blue sky." Eddie turned and loped along with Mike towards the far edge of Old Lady Lauffer's yard.

He cast a quick glance at the Lauffer house, hoping she wasn't watching them. The fact that they both held fishing equipment plainly revealed their intention to fish from her property. The only pond within walking distance sat in the wooded valley that swept behind her back yard. Though she had always seemed kind enough to Eddie, they both knew she had called the cops on trespassers in the past.

Old Lady Lauffer owned the woods that lined their back yards and encircled their cul-de-sac, including the pond. Mike's father had told them her property wrapped all the way around their entire suburban development. An impressive golf course comprised the center of the development, with sections of the course dividing the neighborhood into clusters of streets and houses. As the president of the Sutter Valley Country Club, Mike's dad had tried several times to buy portions of her land to expand the golf course. She had refused every offer. Eddie couldn't understand why, since she rarely ventured into her own backyard. Why would she care about how much property she owned? On the other hand, she didn't appear to need additional money. Though she lived alone, her palatial home dwarfed the others on their street, and her driveway had hosted a number of high-end luxury vehicles over the years.

As soon as the Lauffer house dropped out of sight behind them, the boys cut through her woods towards the pond. Though a proper trail didn't exist, none was needed. Above their heads, a canopy of tall pine trees blocked out much of the sunlight. They ambled down a shallow slope, almost free of vegetation and undergrowth. The terrain converged on a picturesque creek at the base of the valley. Less than a hundred yards downstream, the creek opened into a serene little pond, roughly an acre or two wide. At the far side of the pond, the water narrowed once again into a bubbling stream that fed through the woods to the golf course. If you looked through the trees, you could just see the edge of one of the fairways. Thick undergrowth had retaken that side of the woods, as well as most of the shoreline around the pond.

"You ever see anybody else back here, Ghetti?" Mike asked, peering through the small gap to the golf course.

As always, Eddie took his old nickname in stride. Back in grade school, his long straggly red hair had earned him the nickname "Eddie Spaghetti." Most of the kids had stopped using it long ago, after he had switched to a more conventional hair style. Mike still used his familiar contraction of "Ghetti," however, when they weren't at school.

"One time I saw a couple of old guys eyeballing the pond when they were looking for a lost ball, but I don't think anybody even knows it's back here. From the course, it just looks like a swamp in the woods. Besides, with the big lake just a few miles away, anybody who's really into fishing would just go there."

"Yeah, probably right. Lucky for us!" Mike plunked his tackle box down and uncapped his rod case.

"So, dude, great to finally see you again. How did soccer go this year?" Eddie asked. Eddie didn't have much interest in high school sports, but he wanted to get a conversation going so he could ask Mike a few more interesting questions without raising suspicion.

"Pretty good, actually. Didn't win sectionals, but we got farther in playoffs than we did last year."

"Sounds like you had a couple of really good games yourself," Eddie said. His mother had twice saved the front page of the local paper's sports section for Mike's family. Both pages displayed huge pictures of Mike executing dramatic shots on goal.

In spite of Eddie's general disinterest in sports, he envied Mike's cool appearance in the pictures. While the harried defensemen looked panicked and clumsy, Mike embodied the calm, focused poise of a professional athlete. Even while horizontal in the air for his heroic kicks, not one hair on his head fell out of place. And my God, the girls loved him! Though he never seemed to settle on a long-term favorite, Mike always had at least one lovely lass walking with him or holding his hand in the hallway. Eddie couldn't even imagine what that must feel like.

"I snuck in a few lucky shots," Mike answered. "Our whole offense rocked this year. Hopefully even better next year."

"Yes, I heard you were extremely offensive, in fact. Bad breath, maybe?"

"Bite me, Ghetti!" Mike grinned and whipped the plastic rod case cap at Eddie's head.

"Come on, you set yourself up for that. And what's this I hear about Geoff going out with Cindy?" Even as he said it, Eddie knew he had jumped to this question too soon. Based on Mike's startled reaction, he wondered if maybe he had suddenly realized Eddie's infatuation. But Eddie just had to know. He'd heard rumors that Geoff St. Vincent was either already going out with Cindy, or at least had plans to do so. Like Mike, Geoff was one of the "cool kid" jocks in their class that pretty much owned the school. But unlike Mike, Geoff enjoyed picking on smaller guys to boost his own status even further. Eddie felt certain that if Geoff had any interest in Cindy, his own chances of ever dating her would drop to zilch.

"Where did you hear about Geoff and Cindy?" Mike asked. To almost anyone else, Mike's question would have sounded natural and calm. But Eddie knew Mike well enough to know he was seriously pissed. He'd adopted a "thousand-yard stare," and spoke through clenched teeth.

"I...I'm not even sure," stammered Eddie. "Just something I heard in the hallway. But I heard it more than once. I kinda figured it was just a rumor, but I didn't know for sure."

"He's full of shit, Ghetti. She sees right through douchebags like him."

"That's cool. I figured he probably made it up. She's way too good for him."

Mike shot him a funny look, as though for the first time he may have understood why Eddie cared so much about Cindy's love life.

"That's for sure," Mike finally said. He walked past Eddie to grab his rod case cap from the thick carpet of pine needles. "So, you ready to fish, Ghetti, or are we just gonna gab like an old ladies' knitting club all morning?"

Both boys considered themselves pure anglers, and as such refused to use live bait. Eddie would switch between a weighted artificial worm and a collection of small spoons and spinners. Mike had the same setups for his own spinning rod, but he would also try his fly rod on occasion. His grandfather had given it to him a few years ago. Using the fly rod proved challenging, due to low branches surrounding the pond. That project usually ended in frustration, swearing, and lost dry flies. Frustrations aside, Mike still insisted on trying a few casts with it whenever he went to the pond. Eddie had to admit, it did look impressive when Mike would cast with the fly rod. Almost like a martial art.

Eddie made his way towards a grassy peninsula that jutted out into the center of the pond. He often caught good-sized bluegills and bass from this spot, especially when casting just short of the cattails on the far side. Mike passed behind him to get to his own favorite spot, a wider area closer to the creek outlet on the downstream side. The spots were close enough so they could talk, but far enough away that they wouldn't interfere with each other's lines.

Eddie's first cast landed exactly where he aimed, just short of the cattails. He waited a moment for the lure to sink, then began to slowly jig and reel the line back in. Almost instantly, his line twitched with a firm tap. Nice! To give his quarry another chance, he stopped jigging to let the lure settle. After a few long seconds, he was rewarded with a solid strike. He set the hook and could tell right away that he'd hooked a good one. A bright green-yellow flash zipped just below the surface.

"Got one," he announced, trying not to sound too excited.

"Already? Jeez, I'm not even set up yet!" Mike dropped his gear to watch the fight.

The line arced back and forth, spanning more than half the width of the pond. He had the drag set low, based on the size of his usual catches. The low drag allowed the line to be pulled back off the reel several times, creating a theatric see-saw battle of man versus beast. But he didn't dare mess with the drag now. As he worked the fish closer into the shallow water, he laid eyes on a monster bass -- the biggest he'd ever seen in this pond. He wished he'd brought his net.

"Holy cow, Ghetti. Nice one! Don't lose him!" Mike was already jogging over to assist, if needed.

Eddie had reeled in as much line as he dared and prepared for the critical moment. He had lost more than a few fish during this touchy transition. Keeping the rod tip high, he grabbed the leader with his free hand and eased the bass onto the grassy shore. As he stepped backwards, he tripped and almost stumbled on something in a clump of tall grass. He regained his footing, hooked his finger through the bass's gills and displayed his catch to Mike.

"Damn! He's gotta be four pounds at least. I'm gonna catch his big brother!" Mike turned back to his fishing spot while Eddie clipped the bass onto his stringer. He looped the other end of the stringer around a low branch and dropped his catch back in the water. The big bass flopped in vain, held fast by the stringer. Should be enough for his mother and himself for dinner, he figured, but another good size one would be more than welcome. He checked his lure and prepared for another cast.

As Eddie wound up to cast, his eye caught the object in the grass he had stumbled over. He had forgotten about it in all the excitement. It looked like a computer bag that a professional businessman would carry. What the hell would it be doing out here? Setting his rod down, he picked the bag out of the tuft of grass. The bag felt light, and Eddie guessed it probably held nothing. He opened the two plastic clasps anyway. Couldn't hurt to check. Sure enough, a thin notebook-sized computer occupied the main pocket. In the smaller pocket he found a power cord and a folded sheet of paper.

"Hey Mike," he shouted. "Check this out!" Just the thought of owning a new computer thrilled Eddie. He shared an outdated desktop computer with his mother. Even if they could afford high speed internet service, the ancient processor would have struggled to keep up. Just basic e-mail and periodic access to school websites seemed to push their home PC to its limit. The intense high-res graphic games that his classmates enjoyed were out of the question. But if this thing worked, he would finally have a decent computer of his own. What a day!

"Whatcha got?" Mike looked up from his fly rod, still not quite assembled.

"It's a laptop bag. With a laptop!"

"It was just sitting there?" Mike squinted and started over to inspect the strange find.

"Yeah, tucked into that little clump of grass," Eddie pointed. He opened the folded paper, hoping it didn't contain a return address. If it did belong to somebody, he supposed he would have to "do the right thing" and return it to its owner. But who would leave a laptop out here? It's not like this was a bus stop or a restaurant. To his surprise, the paper read like an invitation… or a challenge. He read through the message while Mike inspected the bag's side pockets. Finding nothing else, Mike picked up the laptop, but was unable to open it.

"It looks like my dad's MAC notebook, but the latches are different," he said. "And there's no 'Apple' logo."

Seeing the confused look on Eddie's face, Mike put the laptop down and read from the paper himself.

## GREETINGS, HOODLUM!

## DO YOU HAVE WHAT IT TAKES TO MEET THE HOODLUM CHALLENGE?

If so, you will be rewarded in cash! If not, please leave the bag, computer and instructions as you found them for the next Hoodlum to find.

To play this game, use the laptop computer to direct you through the challenges. The computer has been modified to only support this application; it will not work as a functional computer. If you attempt to modify the software or remove the laptop covers, the hard drive will be wiped and the game is over.

## Playing the Game

1. The Hoodlum game consists of a series of challenges. For each challenge you will be given a task to complete. Each task will list a monetary award to be paid in full when the task has been completed and verified.

2. At any time during each task, you may be observed by the Hoodlum Gamemaster. You will not be aware of this; it is merely to ensure you are complying with the rules of the game and to verify the successful completion of each task.

3. To play Hoodlum you may involve one <u>and only one</u> other individual to assist you. If the Hoodlum Gamemaster observes more than one assistant involved in the task, the challenge award will be forfeit and no further tasks will be offered. Be sure that your partner is someone that you can trust!

4. You (and your partner, if you choose to use one) must not reveal to any other person that you are playing Hoodlum. If the Gamemaster learns that you have revealed the secret to anyone else, the challenge

award will be forfeit and no further tasks will be offered.

5. Be advised: The individual tasks may involve breaking the law. If you are caught by the authorities, the hard drive will be wiped remotely. You will <u>not</u> be able to use the Hoodlum game or any of its rules to defend yourself or your partner from legal action. Take a moment to seriously consider this before accepting the challenge.

If you do accept these rules and risks, Bravo! To unlock the laptop, push outward on the two front latches and hold for five seconds. Good luck, and show us what you can do!

Respectfully,

*The Hoodlum Gamemaster*

Eddie waited for Mike to finish reading. He would have preferred a free computer of his own, but he felt intrigued by the strange challenge.

"Gotta be some kind of prank, right?" he asked, almost laughing when he saw Mike's baffled expression.

"Damn Ghetti, I don't know. It seems like almost anything you do wipes out the hard drive."

"Yeah," agreed Eddie. "I noticed that. Pretty clear that it's got to be a complete secret."

"What possible reason could someone have to do this? Just to get somebody in a shitload of trouble? Must be some stupid reality TV thing." Mike gave the paper back to Eddie and picked up the computer for a closer inspection.

"And why would they leave it here, of all places?" asked Eddie. "Far as I know, we're the only ones that ever come down here. It's like it was meant for us to find."

Mike seemed to contemplate this for a moment. He looked around, as though the Gamemaster might be watching them even now.

"Good point. There's no way it could have been left here for anyone but us. We're the only ones who probably even know about this place, right?"

"You think maybe Geoff, or one of his jackass friends?" Eddie offered. "Those guys know that we fish back here somewhere, but I don't think they know exactly where the pond is. Most of those guys live near the clubhouse, on the other side of the course."

"I wouldn't put it past him to *want* to do something like this," offered Mike, "but he probably can't even spell computer, much less think up something this wild. Same for the clowns he hangs out with."

"Maybe Old Lady Lauffer? She's probably figured out that we go fishing down here."

Mike rolled his eyes. "Seriously, Ghetti? Why would an old lady set up something like this? And if she's anything like my grandmother, she's probably not too swift at using computers, either."

"Could be she's just bored," Eddie suggested. "Or maybe she hired somebody to set this up on us. Even the name 'Hoodlum' sounds like something an old person would say."

"Maybe. But why? If she's pissed about us fishing down here, she could have busted us red-handed dozens of times. She knows my dad would kill me if I did anything to blow his big land deal with her."

"I thought she refused to sell. Did he raise the offer?"

"No, but he's always trying to kiss her ass to win her over. Free club membership for life, open tab for the dining room, that kind of crap. Like she would ever use it."

"Well, whoever it is, it's still got to be some kind of prank, right?"

"It doesn't make any sense, Ghetti. Prank or not."

"Well, should we try it out? I mean, we could open it up and just see what kind of things they ask us to do. If it's really crazy, we stuff it back in the bag and keep fishing, right?"

Mike sighed and skimmed the rules again. "I guess that would be OK. Unless this thing sprays paint or something all over us when we open it. Maybe that's the prank."

Eddie laughed, imagining themselves getting spritzed with paint or fart spray.

"Good thought. We'll at least open it up and start it pointed away from us."

Mike took a deep breath, pointed the opening side of the laptop away from himself, and followed the directions to unlatch the computer. To the relief of both boys, the laptop opened with no surprises.

With the screen still pointed away, Eddie reached around and pressed the power button. They could see the screen flash to life, and again no spray or explosion. Mike twisted the laptop around so both of them could see the display.

The border of the bright screen showed a number of ominous symbols: a satanic five-pointed star, the Hazmat radioactive material sign, sticks of dynamite with a burning fuse, a skull and cross bones and several others.

In the center of the screen in large font, the message "Congratulations, and Welcome to Hoodlum – A Game for the Truly Bold!" flashed between dark and light text.

Beneath that, in smaller font, the message "Press to reveal your first task – if you dare!" hovered over a virtual button.

"Well, we've gone this far," said Eddie. Let's see what it is."

Mike waggled his head back and forth, glanced at Eddie, slid the cursor to the button and pressed. The main screen disappeared and a second took its place.

At the top of the screen, "Task Reward = $200" stood highlighted above a paragraph of specific instructions.

**Your first challenge is to "modify" the 30 MPH speed limit sign near the main entrance to the Sutter Valley community. A bag with everything you need is concealed behind the spotlight for the Sutter Valley entrance sign. Use the contents of the bag to modify the sign appropriately – any Hoodlum worth his salt will know exactly what to do. Remember the rules, and good luck!**

Mike looked at Eddie when he finished reading.

"This has gotta be the weirdest thing I've ever seen. It must be some kind of setup." Mike shook his head in obvious disapproval of the whole venture.

Perhaps he still felt jazzed by the thrill of his big bass, but Eddie wanted to talk this through. He knew they both could use the money, perhaps more so than the average high school kids. Eddie's job at the local supermarket paid well enough for all the hours he put in, but a good portion of that went to help his mother out with the bills. And Mike's sports schedule left him no time at all for a job. He depended on his meager allowance for personal expenses.

"Come on, let's just plan it out," Eddie pleaded. "Even if we don't actually do it, it's kind of like a puzzle to figure it out. That's not a crime."

"OK, Ghetti. I'm game. How would we do it?" Mike plopped the open laptop down on its case and sat in the grass.

Eddie could tell that Mike would need some serious convincing. He knew that Mike valued his reputation with his family and friends above all else. But he also knew that Mike loved a challenge as much as he did, so maybe he still had a chance.

"This'll be easy," said Eddie. "We wait until dark and pull our bikes right up to the sign, like the chain slipped off or something. We prop the bike against the sign. One of us watches for headlights, the other guy stands on the bike frame and works on the sign. Nothin' to it."

"You're assuming the gamekeeper, or whatever, doesn't want us to get caught. What if he *does* want that? Maybe that's the prank. To bust us in the middle of the night trying to vandalize road signs for a hundred friggin' bucks each."

"OK, I agree that's a slim possibility. So we'll be extra careful. We'll cruise around the entrance on our bikes first, and check the area for cars, cameras or whatever else before we even go for the bag, right?"

Mike drooped his head, then a thought seemed to occur to him.

"You're not thinking of doing this alone, are you? Dude, you could really get in a lot of trouble. The last thing you need is to get busted junior year. Some stupid thing like this could trash your whole future."

"Mike, I promise I won't do this unless you agree. I'm just trying to think of how we *could* do it, if we wanted to."

"Well Jesus, you've already got this pretty well planned out. Are you the Gamekeeper?"

"Gamemaster. And no. If I had a computer like this, I woulda just kept it." Eddie laughed. Did Mike really think he would know how to set something like this up? He loved computer games and had a solid knack for basic programming, but he had no idea how to create such a sophisticated application.

"Come on, Mike. Even if we did get caught, how much trouble would we really be in? A speed limit sign. Hardly the crime of the century."

Mike covered his eyes with his hands and fell back on the grass.

"I'll probably regret this," he said, "but let's do it."

## Chapter 2 - The First Task: A Natural Hoodlum

Back in the kitchen, Eddie spread old newspapers on the counter to clean his fish. He'd added two fat bluegills to the stringer after finding the Hoodlum laptop. More than enough for dinner with his mother.

On any other day, mentally reliving his great catch would have been enough. Today, however, the Hoodlum game dominated his thoughts. The whole thing seemed surreal. If Mike hadn't been there to share the experience, he may have doubted that it had even happened. But it did! He couldn't stop thinking about the promise of cash rewards. He tried not to get too excited, though. For all he knew, they'd never see a dime of the money. But real or not, the game had captured his full attention.

When he finished prepping the fish, Eddie opened the fridge to store the plate of fillets for dinner. He smiled when he noticed a new fortune cookie message magnetized to the door.

Assorted calendars, coupons, post-it-notes and Eddie's academic awards cluttered the front of the refrigerator, but his mother kept a small spot near the handle clear. She would often post amusing fortune cookie messages in this reserved little square. The newest one read "The early bird gets the worm, but the second mouse gets the cheese." That certainly had a profound ring to it. They both loved Chinese food, and sharing their fortunes had been part of the tradition since he was in grade school.

She had permanently taped her all-time favorite an inch or so above the new one. The faded text declared "Your future is an unwritten page, for YOU are the author of your own destiny." To Eddie, that one seemed a little corny, but he understood why she liked it.

---

Tina, Eddie's mother, sat back from her empty plate and gazed at him. She had a pretty face, but her eyes looked as though she hadn't slept in days.

"That was some dinner, Eddie. Great catch, and a great dinner. Did you get a picture of the big bass before you filleted him?"

"Yeah, Mike took a couple of me holding him. He's going to print 'em out for me." Eddie didn't want to dwell on the fact that he was probably the only one in his class that didn't have a smart phone with a camera. He knew she wanted him to have nice things, but they just couldn't afford one. They both had pay-as-you-go phones. Eddie went to great lengths at school to avoid letting any of his classmates see it.

"That's nice, Hon. And you got the whole kitchen cleaned up, too. I really appreciate it, after the long week I had."

"I know, Mom. I wish you didn't have to work so many hours."

"Me too. But it'll pay off when I get the promotion." She grabbed his waist as he walked by with an armload of dirty dishes and gave him a tight hug.

It seemed like his mother forever talked about the "next big promotion." Sometimes she wouldn't get it, and other times she'd get the promotion but there would be some other setback -- not as much pay as she had been told, or an unexpected home repair. As hard as she worked, she never seemed to get ahead. Apart from their dinners together, and watching TV in the evenings on basic cable, her only joy in life was the Friday night outings with her friends from work. She would go to one of the local bars and have a few drinks, and occasionally get in some dancing.

As long as Eddie could remember, she had never gone on a date. He wondered if some of the Friday nights, particularly the ones when she'd gotten home *very* late, if that's what she was up to. If so, she never mentioned anything about it to him. He guessed she just felt awkward talking to him about her love life, but he hoped that she would eventually find someone. The thought of her living alone and just working forever troubled him deeply.

Eddie had never known his father, or even knew much about the man at all. Based on his mother's reactions whenever he asked, he got the sense that she had gotten pregnant very young, and most likely by someone she barely knew. Over the years he had stopped asking altogether, though he yearned to learn more. He loved his mother enough to not push her on the matter. She had sacrificed a great deal to raise him on her own, and he didn't want her to feel guilty about it. God knows, they had been through some tough times together.

"And how 'bout you, Eddie Bear?" she asked. "Still kickin' ass on the grades? Junior year is the big one for getting scholarships, you know."

"I'm doing OK, Mom." In truth, Eddie was ranked number four in his class, despite his tough load of advanced classes. He found that getting good grades came pretty easily to him. His guidance counselor told him he had a solid shot for scholarships at some top-notch schools. Part of him wanted to take advantage of that. But he knew that going to school meant leaving his mother behind and taking away his part of the household income for at least four years. Even with a full scholarship and a campus job, college would cost both of them dearly.

"Your grandpa would be so proud of you," she said. "You still thinking about engineering?"

"I think so. I haven't decided yet." This wasn't a complete lie. He hadn't told his mother, but he had been talking to military recruiters at school. He knew that bringing this up would restart their usual argument, but he wanted to hash this out.

"I did really well on some tests for the Navy and Air Force," he said. He watched his mother draw a deep breath, already preparing to shut him down. "I can pretty much get any enlisted job I want, guaranteed."

"Eddie, we talked about this. You know there are no guarantees in the military. They just want to get you to sign up, and you'll be stuck. You'll be scraping paint, washing dishes or driving a truck while your friends all get college degrees!"

"I won't be scraping paint, Mom. I'll be learning electronics and getting real hands-on experience. When I get out, I can use the GI bill to pay for college, and I'd be getting paid as soon as I finish high school."

"But your grades are already good enough to get your college paid for. Now is your best shot at getting into a good school, and you really deserve to go. If you put it off, like I did, you may never get another chance."

"The scholarships won't pay for everything, Mom. It's still going to cost a ton of money."

"Remember what your grandfather said. He got his engineering degree first, then went in to the Army as an officer. He wasn't a millionaire, but he did very well and retired with a good pension. And he left us enough money to pay off our house and get a decent car."

"I know what Grandpa did, Mom. I'm just saying that may not be the only way to do it. Or the best way."

"We can take out loans if we need to, Eddie, but we'll work it out. I promise. Please don't do anything more with the recruiters without telling me first, OK?"

"I won't do anything without telling you, but I want you keep an open mind about this. Deal?"

"Deal. Seal the deal with some team Ponzino dishwashing?" Tina raised her fist.

Eddie returned her fist bump and started to collect the dishes. He felt as though he had gained some ground in their eternal argument for the first time. And given their circumstances, he really *did* think his grandfather would be proud of him.

He loaded the dishwasher while his mother washed the frying pan and pots. She swayed to Steely Dan's "Aja" as she dried and stored them, trying to get Eddie to dance along with her. He smiled, but continued to wipe the counters and table.

"I'm still really beat," Tina said as they finished. "I might read for a bit, but no TV for me tonight. I'd be out in two seconds. Thanks again for the great dinner, Eddie." She reached into her purse on the counter and pulled out a paperback.

"So, I guess it'll be sci-fi and gore for me tonight, eh?" he smirked. When they watched movies together, she would often remind him that those were not her favorite genres.

"You go right ahead with that garbage." She popped him lightly on the head with her book. "Just don't stay up too late, zombie killer!"

As soon as she yawned and kissed him goodnight, he snuck out the back door.

---

Mike and Eddie had already moved their bikes from their garages to the hidden space next to Eddie's shed. Though it was still well before his weekend curfew, Mike worried that his parents might call him in if they saw him rolling down the driveway on his bike after sunset. One of his teammates had gotten hit by a car while biking after dark last summer. Though the kid recovered with no permanent injuries, Mike's mother seemed convinced that her son would be next.

Once it got just dark enough, they walked the bikes around the far side of Eddie's house to loop past Mike's house undetected. Eddie's mother would be fast asleep by now, and probably wouldn't have stopped him anyway. He knew she cared about him deeply; he simply had never given her any reason to worry. As they buzzed by Mike's house on the far side of the street, they could see the rest of his family through the living room window watching TV. Good to go!

Because their quiet little street defined the midpoint of the Sutter Valley development, the ride to the neighborhood entrance only took a few minutes. During rush hour on weekdays, school busses, minivans and SUVs would paralyze this little tee intersection. But on a Saturday night at this hour, hardly any traffic passed near the entrance at all.

A beautifully landscaped brick edifice formed the backdrop of the "Sutter Valley Community and Country Club" sign. The letters themselves stood out from the background in lavish wrought iron script. The pompous-looking entrance always made Eddie laugh. Every time they drove by it, his mother would raise her nose in the air and pronounce the name with a garishly snobby accent. Never got old.

A canned spotlight squatted off to the right lower corner of the brick wall to illuminate the sign after dark. You'd hate to think that someone might drive by at night and not realize what a fabulous place they were passing!

The boys coasted through the entrance and rode a short distance down the highway in both directions. No parked cars either way, and no obvious signs of cameras or anything else in the wooded tree line. Eddie even checked out the thick brush on the opposite side, directly across from the entrance. If someone really wanted to bust them in the act, Eddie supposed this would be the ideal vantage point. He spooked a doe just inside the thicket, which he took as a good sign. Not likely anyone else could stalk them from this spot without scaring the doe off earlier. He crossed back over to begin the challenge.

"Whattya think?" Mike asked.

Even in the darkness Eddie could sense Mike's nervousness. His head swiveled back and forth, looking for lights or movement of any kind.

"Looks good. No sign of anyone watching that I can see."

"I dunno, Ghetti. They could be watching us from a half mile away on some telescopic lens camera, or whatever. Probably laughing their asses off already."

Eddie chuckled to himself. This Mike seemed very different from the "grace under pressure" athlete from the front page of the Sports section. He didn't want to make him even more nervous by acting reckless, though.

"Even if it is a reality tv setup, let's at least look like pros. I don't mind doing the dirty work, as long as I can count on you to look for cars. Are you good with that?"

This seemed to ease Mike's concern somewhat. He nodded his consent, and Eddie dismounted to collect the bag of supplies.

Eddie propped his bike up against the brick wall, checked both ways for cars, and strode right up to the spotlight. As promised, a small canvas sack sat just barely covered in mulch at the base of the light. He shook the mulch off the bag and brought it into the beam to take a look. The bag contained only two items, a small can of black spray paint and a cardboard stencil cutout of the number "three."

Mike had ridden back up the road a short distance but doubled back when he realized Eddie already had the bag. He checked for cars, then joined Eddie to inspect the vandalism kit.

"What the hell are we supposed to do with that?" he asked. "The task thing said a true hoodlum would know what to do."

"I got this," Eddie said, smiling. "Just watch for cars, OK?"

An interesting thought occurred to him. For once, he had emerged as the leader of their whole game plan. It went without saying that Mike called the shots when they did pretty much anything together. In truth, he never minded, or even noticed until now. It felt pretty cool to run the show.

Eddie pushed his bike fifty feet or so through the entrance. He stopped and looked up at his objective. Beneath the official "30 MPH" speed limit sign, another sign cautioned "Please Drive Slowly – Children at Play." He figured if he leaned his bike at just the right angle, he could stand on the frame just under the seat and have perfect access to the sign.

Eddie had not expected to feel so relaxed during the task. It also gave him a little blast of bravado that he knew instinctively what to do to the sign, while Mike appeared to be clueless.

Eddie didn't consider himself a saint by any means, but he had never done anything like this. He knew that spoiled rich kids didn't mind damaging property for whatever reason, but he had always thought of vandalism as wasteful and stupid. It surprised him that he genuinely wanted to do this, and not just for the money. Was it the excitement of planning and executing the caper, or the idea of becoming a criminal for the first time? Maybe both? He took a moment to look around and remember every sensation.

Mike had ridden to the halfway point between the entrance and the speed limit sign. Prior to grabbing the bag, they had determined that this was the best spot to watch for headlights from all directions. Though less likely, it had occurred to them that someone might be leaving rather than driving by or entering the neighborhood at this hour. They would need to cover that possibility, too, so Mike had to stay on the neighborhood side of the entrance.

"Headlights, Ghetti!" Mike somehow yelled and whispered at the same time. Eddie bent over his bike, as though inspecting the rear sprocket and derailleur. After a moment, the car hissed by on the main road.

"Clear," Mike said. Eddie rolled his bike forward and leaned it against the sign. Holding the stencil in one hand, he clambered up his bike frame to face the sign directly. The "three" cut out in the stencil perfectly matched the "three" in the 30 MPH sign, as he hoped. Yes! He knew exactly what to do. He shook the paint can and pressed the stencil against the sign.

"Headlights, Ghetti! From inside!" Mike warned. He pushed his bike up towards Eddie's to support the breakdown charade.

Eddie could already see the approaching glow of the headlights from behind the sign. He dropped to the ground and resumed his bike repair pose. He could feel his heartbeat pounding as the car slowed to stop beside them.

"Need any help?" the driver yelled through the open window. Eddie cringed. They knew just about everyone in the community. He did not want to be recognized by a neighbor near the sign. That would move him right to the top of the suspect list once their crime went public.

"No thanks – chain just slipped off!" he waved the driver on without lifting his head above the bike's rear wheel.

The driver waved back and pulled away while another car passed on the main road. Mike shook his head and made a stressed whistling sound, as though the task seemed impossible. As soon as the second car had passed, Eddie waved Mike back to his spotter position. He quickly repositioned his bike against the signpost, climbed up and got ready to work. It was a little trickier than he thought to balance against the post and hold the stencil in one hand and the can of paint in the other. He rotated the cut out "three" to form a mirror image of the three on the sign, then sprayed as smoothly as he could while wobbling on the bike. After a few precarious moments, he pulled the stencil away and admired his work. Not perfect, but pretty damn good, given the conditions.

He dropped down to the ground and waved Mike over. Mike took a quick look around for cars, rode over and shined the flashlight from his phone on the sign. He broke into a huge grin and whacked Eddie on the back.

"You are a natural goddam hoodlum, Ghetti! 80 miles an hour. That's awesome! And it looks so clean, I bet it'll take people a while to notice."

"Works for me! As long as the Gamemaster notices." Eddie flushed with pride at the compliment. He could see a blotch of black spray paint on the back of his left hand, where he'd held the stencil.

"Speaking of that, did you recognize the guy that stopped?" asked Mike.

"No, did you?" Eddie hadn't even considered that the guy in the passing car could have been the Gamemaster.

"It looked like the Austins' Odyssey, with the ski rack, but that wasn't Billy's dad. I have no idea."

"Well, I guess our job here is done," Eddie said. "What should we do with this?" he held up the canvas bag with the paint and stencil. "Probably shouldn't show up in our trash cans."

"We'll just swing by the middle school on the way back and whip it in the dumpster."

The boys mounted up to ride home. Eddie wished it was just a little bit brighter so he could take another good look at his handiwork. Man, it felt great to be a badass!

# The Hoodlum Game

## Chapter 3 - The Second Task: One Mermaid to Go!

Just like the morning before, Eddie couldn't wait to get out of the house. He did take the time to toast a pair of frozen waffles, but wolfed them down in seconds. Had anyone seen the sign yet? Someone would probably notice it on their drive home from church. Would they really get paid for completing the challenge, or were they just naïve idiots? The suspense was killing him, but he promised Mike last night he would wait for him before checking the laptop again.

When they had first returned from the fishing venture, they had stuffed the Hoodlum laptop, case and all, into a bucket in Eddie's shed. Last night, after defacing the sign, they had ducked back into the shed to check. Neither of them expected confirmation of the completion of the first task so quickly, but they checked anyway. If the Gamemaster had confirmed, the laptop gave no indication. It had displayed the same information as before, still daring them to complete the first task.

Eddie had pointed out that it would've been a little creepier if the task *had* been confirmed already. That would mean the Gamemaster had been watching them in real time. Mike agreed, and made Eddie promise not to check again without him.

Now Eddie regretted making the promise. The Ashland family attended church every Sunday, and Mike had made it known that today would be no exception. That meant waiting until at least eleven a.m. for their return, and that's assuming Mrs. Ashland didn't linger to socialize. And as Mike had said last night, "Good luck with that."

Eddie cleaned up his breakfast and looked at the clock. Jesus. At least two hours to go. He should have told Mike to sneak over before church, so they could've checked again before he left. He supposed it didn't matter -- if the game was legit, they would still get paid. He thought about going fishing again but changed his mind. His mother had started on their weekly laundry, so he folded the load from the dryer and tossed in a new batch from the washer. To his dismay, that little diversion only used up seven minutes.

He wanted to see the speed limit sign in the bright light of day. Besides, a little sightseeing excursion just might take up enough time to keep him from breaking his promise to Mike.

The peaceful sounds of the birds and cicadas in the trees helped him relax as he coasted back to the scene of the crime. He didn't see any traffic around the entrance, so he felt safe enough to stop and stare directly at the sign for a moment. But no longer than a moment, he warned himself. Though he had scrubbed vigorously, a residual dusting of black paint still covered the back of his left hand and wrist. Not a big deal if anyone noticed, unless he was spotted directly beneath the vandalized road sign admiring his work.

Mike had called it well. The modified "eight" looked naturally symmetric, and the finish on the black spray paint matched the rest of the sign perfectly. You could see a thin black dribble at the bottom of the "eight," but you had to look hard to see it. He wondered if people would catch the absurd speed limit change, or would just drive by it without even noticing such a well-blended alteration to the numbers they had passed so many times before. Someone would pick up on it eventually. And once they did, he imagined everyone would check it out.

Though he didn't want to get in any "official" trouble for this, a small part of him hoped that word might somehow get around that it was his idea. Eddie knew that this act alone could not propel him into the "Cool Kid" ranks, but it just might move him up another rung or two on the long social ladder. He shrugged and started the trip back home to wait for Mike.

---

Eddie's watch showed 11:35 when the Ashland's car rolled up the driveway. He sat reading in one of the plastic deck chairs on his own front porch. His physics teacher had loaned him an interesting magazine about careers in Robotics and

Artificial Intelligence. Normally Eddie would have devoured this stuff, but today he couldn't read more than a page or two without his thoughts drifting back to the Hoodlum game. Thank God they had finally returned!

"Hey, Mr. and Mrs. Ashland! How ya doing, Cindy?" he greeted the Ashlands as they poured out of their SUV.

Mr. Ashland said nothing, but grinned and pretended to shoot Eddie, using his hand as a pistol. Per their long-standing tradition, Eddie pretended to take a gut shot and slumped over in his chair. Holy cow, how many years had they been doing that little routine?

"Oh, hello Edward," Mrs. Ashland answered. "How are you and your mom doing?"

"We're doing fine, thanks." Eddie replied. Her greeting sounded sincere, but Eddie thought she seemed distracted.

"Hey Eddie," Cindy added with only a passing glance in his direction. She followed her parents up their driveway while Mike and Eddie jogged to the back yard.

"Michael?" his mother called. "Don't forget to change out of your church clothes!"

"I won't, Mom," Mike answered, but stayed right on Eddie's heels.

Eddie felt embarrassed about the shed, even more so now that it had become headquarters for the Hoodlum game. Another proud feature of the "Ponzino Estate," the shed had once looked like a miniature red barn. He remembered handing his grandfather tools as his "little helper" on the shed project so many years ago.

Now, the thin metal walls and roof showed more rust than paint, and the flimsy doors drooped so badly they couldn't even close. Eddie had fashioned a functional but crude door latch from a bent coat hanger. He unhooked the latch and creaked the doors open. As they entered into the darkness, a blast of muggy air nearly pushed them back out. The place reeked of rotting grass clippings, spent fertilizer and stale gas. On top of that, there wasn't enough room for either of them to sit. The computer bag sat tucked inside a plastic grass seed bucket. Eddie pulled it out and placed it so they could both see the screen as it powered up.

"Congratulations!" beamed the display. "You have successfully completed the first task! To claim your cash reward, go to the tee area for hole number four of the golf course. You will find an unmarked envelope with the reward fastened to the underside of the ball washer. Please collect your reward to activate the next challenge." The "Proceed to Next Task" virtual button below the instructions appeared to be disabled. It looked like a thin, hazy version of itself.

"Great," said Mike, shaking his head. "The course is probably packed with golfers today. Now we gotta grab the envelope right in front of a crowd of people. That won't look too suspicious."

"We should be able to just zip in there and grab it. Your dad is the Prez, right? Who can stop us? And if anyone is hanging around waiting to tee off, one of us could just cause a distraction or something. Come on, compared to what we already did, this'll be a snap!"

"All right," he finally said. "I gotta change my clothes first."

Less than twenty minutes later the boys sped down the golf course cart path on their bikes. Except for an angry shout from a startled golf cart driver, no one seemed to care. As Mike predicted, golfers seemed to crowd every hole on the course. He had brought along an old radio control transmitter. If stopped or questioned, he figured he could tell them that he'd lost his R/C plane.

To Mike's relief, they arrived at the hole four tee between groups and grabbed the envelope unnoticed. Eddie couldn't resist peeking inside to check. Yes! The thrilling glimpse of cash! He jumped back on his bike without counting it, and they pedaled back to Eddie's garage at a leisurely pace.

Eddie noticed that his mom's car was gone. Probably grocery shopping. They coasted up the driveway and dismounted before even coming to a stop. Mike nearly collided with an old chaise lounge in the cluttered Ponzino garage but stuck the landing. Eddie already had the envelope out to count the cash.

"It's all here, Dude – we did it!" He handed Mike five twenties. "Not bad for a quick evening's work, eh?"

Mike followed Eddie through the back door of his garage to the shed. The rest of the Ashland family sat scattered around the pool and deck. They didn't seem to notice that the boys had even left at all.

They ducked inside and powered up the laptop once again. The previously grayed-out "Proceed to Next Task" button was now active, and Eddie pressed it without even giving Mike a chance to argue.

"Ghetti, wait!" Mike looked as though Eddie had just pulled the pin on a grenade.

"Relax, Mike. Now we know it's not a scam. We'll check out the next task, just like last time. If it looks too risky, we bag it. No harm done, right?"

"We can see what the next task is, but it still could be a scam. That first one could just be a way to make us let our guard down for the next one. And here's something else to think about - - the Gamemaster must've seen us collect the cash just a few minutes ago. Why else would that next task button be enabled already? Whoever is doing this is watching us close; maybe all the time! We gotta be really careful, Ghetti. This whole stupid thing still doesn't make sense."

Eddie shook his head and positioned the laptop so they could both read the details of the next challenge. Before revealing the specifics, the top of the screen flashed four hundred dollars as the next task reward.

The task itself involved stealing the mermaid statue from the Lauffers' fountain. The instructions did not describe how to go about the act specifically, nor what to do with the statue once it had been removed. The instructions did suggest breaking or unscrewing the floodlight that illuminated the gardens, however.

"Steal Old Lady Lauffer's mermaid? That's pretty freakin' crazy all right," said Mike. "I'd love to get the cash, but how would we pull off something like that? For all we know, the damn thing weighs five hundred pounds!"

"First of all," Eddie said, "we've got to figure that it can't really be that heavy. The rules said only two people max, right? It can't weigh that much, or we'd never be able to lift it."

Mike shrugged.

"And we already got the tip about the floodlight," Eddie continued. "That'll be easy. I'll watch tonight, and make sure there's only one."

"How will you make sure? And what about motion sensors?"

"After it gets dark, I'll pretend to lose a frisbee or something in her garden and walk all around the fountain. If any other lights turn on, I'll find out real quick."

"All right. But what about getting it out of there and moving it, without making noise? It's way too big for a wheelbarrow."

"You've got that small flatbed trailer that you pull around with your ATV, right?"

"Ghetti, that thing's loud as hell!"

41

"We just need the trailer, not the ATV. We could hook it up to your dad's golf cart. That thing's pretty quiet."

Mike grimaced at the thought of using his father's presidential golf cart. His father took great pride in having a cart of his own in their garage, though he rarely used it for golf. "Sutter Valley Golf Club President" was emblazoned on both sides of the cart, and it even sported a small flag with the club logo. Like royalty, his parents drove it around the neighborhood to dinner parties and cookouts, greeting friends and neighbors along the way. If Mike got busted in any sort of crime, involving his father's beloved golf cart would seal his doom forever.

"Sure, Ghetti. Great plan. I guess that means I'll be keeping the stolen statue in my garage, then? That should be a tough crime for the cops to solve. And my parents!"

"No, man. We just gotta figure out somewhere to stash it. Obviously not around our yards, but there's tons of woods around the course. We drive it right down Lauffer's driveway, across the street, then down the access trail to the course. No way for anyone to figure out the tracks; there's hundreds of golf cart tracks there. We go to some other part of the course, back it into the woods and dump it. Even if somebody finds it later, who cares? We still completed the task."

"OK, I guess that might work. But one other thing. How do we know the mermaid isn't glued down to the fountain, or maybe even part of it? Doesn't the water shoot out the top of her head?"

"Yeah, we'll probably need to bring a flashlight and some tools. Maybe bring a scuba mask, if you got one. If we can't do it, we can't do it, and that's that. But two hundred bucks each, Mike. I don't know about you, but I could sure use the cash."

"Me too, but this one seems way tougher than the first one. For all we know, Old Lady Lauffer has nothing else to do but stare out her windows. Even if we're quiet, she's bound to hear us. This whole Hoodlum thing is probably her idea; maybe her way to screw us for fishing in her woods."

"But why would she go to all this trouble?" Eddie asked. "Like you said, she could have nabbed us a hundred times, or just complained to your dad. She knows we'd both be crucified."

"Maybe," Mike said. "I guess we could scope it out tonight before we really do it. But I'm telling you right now - If I see a shadow move inside her house, I'm bailing. Golf cart, trailer and all."

"Fair enough." Eddie agreed. "At least we got Monday off, so no one should care if we're out late again tonight."

Mike made another of his nervous whistling sounds. "OK, Ghetti. See you at 8:30."

---

The shorter autumn days left the back yards along their street in almost total darkness despite the early hour. Eddie took note of the dim quarter moon and light cloud cover, grateful for anything that would help conceal their caper. After leaving the shed in the afternoon, Eddie noticed that the fountain did indeed spray from the top of the mermaid as Mike had claimed. Now, in the growing darkness, he could see the fountain no longer sprayed. Maybe on a timer? At least one thing they wouldn't have to worry about.

Scanning in the opposite direction, he could see Mike crouched behind the hedges that framed their pool. He checked for lights in all three houses. One window on the second floor of Mike's house glowed brightly, but a pulled shade blocked any possible view of the back yards. Mike must have killed the two lights that normally lit the Ashlands' deck. Eddie's mom had gone to bed early again, since she had work tomorrow. No lights from their place at all. The only remaining illumination was the floodlight that covered the Lauffer fountain and surrounding gardens. Perfect!

He joined Mike behind the hedge. Mike already looked stressed. Behind him, the golf cart and flatbed trailer sat waiting for action.

"The friggin' trailer hitch didn't fit," he whispered. "I couldn't get the ball unscrewed from the ATV hitch, so I had to make a cheesy adapter to use it with the golf cart. It'll hold, but no way can we go fast with it."

Eddie checked out the cobbled hitch. Mike had used a pair of c-clamps to keep the tongue from sliding off the undersized ball on the golf cart hitch.

"That's cool," said Eddie. "Slower will be quieter anyway. Did you bring any tools?"

"They're in the golf cart. Full socket set, two big crescent wrenches, vice grips, a hammer and chisel."

Eddie felt a little guilty. Mike must have spent the whole afternoon putting all of this together, and all he brought was an old frisbee that every dog in the neighborhood had tasted over the years.

"Well, here goes the scouting mission." Eddie crept back along the wall of his own house, battered frisbee in hand. He tossed it towards the fountain, then continued across the gap between the houses to the Lauffer yard. He took another look around, then commandoed his way up to the raised patio that overlooked the gardens. Staying beneath the cone of bright light, he moved one of the metal deckchairs to the column with the floodlight. He stood on the chair and reached up to unscrew the bulb. The sudden transformation from bright light to total darkness startled him somewhat, and he froze. Though his eyes hadn't quite adjusted, he scanned the Lauffers' house for any sign of movement. Seeing none, he replaced the chair and started to wander on a wide path around the garden, pretending to look for his wayward frisbee. Still nothing. He flapped his arms and completely circled the fountain, but no other lights turned on. Awesome! He signaled for Mike to join him.

Mike sprinted to the fountain with only the toolbox.

"Aren't ya bringing the cart?" asked Eddie.

"I figured we'd just see if we could get it loose and move it first," Mike whispered. "I'll drive it over when it's ready to load and go."

Eddie agreed that this made sense. He stepped into the fountain, checking the Lauffer house again for any sign of activity. The water felt warmer than he expected, and the depth fell inches below the bottom of his shorts. Wading up to the mermaid, he realized she stood quite a bit taller than he'd thought. He felt around the bottom for any hardware that held the statue in place. He could feel three large nuts around the rim of the base, plus a single threaded fitting where the water supply connected.

He waded back to Mike and asked for the large crescent wrench. The water line fitting removed easily, as did the first of the three anchor nuts. The next nut didn't want to turn at all, probably due to corrosion. Sensing trouble, Mike sloshed up next to him with more tools.

"Did you bring a mask?" asked Eddie, feeling another pang of guilt for having contributed so little.

"I got a pair of Cindy's swimming goggles. That's all I could find."

"Uh, and a flashlight?" Eddie asked, realizing that the goggles would be useless without it.

Mike grinned and produced a small LED penlight. "It's not waterproof, though. I'll hold it for you."

Eddie donned the goggles and settled into the water. So much for dry clothes.

With the help of the light from above, Eddie was able to get a better grip on the stubborn nut with the wrench. After a few tough turns, it spun off. The final nut, however, refused to budge. Mike pushed and pulled on the statue until the base rim around the rusted nut eventually snapped off. He almost lost his grip when the statue broke free, but he made a heroic save.

"Let go of her hooter, ya perv!" Eddie mocked in a whisper.

Mike laughed and groped the mermaid's bare breasts. The mermaid herself appeared to be porcelain or some type of ceramic, molded around a heavy iron base. It may not have weighed the five hundred pounds that Mike had feared, but it would certainly tip the scale at well over one hundred. Together they worked the statue to the side of the fountain and collected the tools. Eddie tossed the frisbee back into his yard, and both boys cringed when it bonked off the back of his house. Still no sign of any reaction to their backyard activities.

To avoid any obvious tracks from their yards, Mike drove the golf cart around the far side of his house, down his driveway, along the street, then up to the fountain from the Lauffers' own driveway. He expertly backed the trailer, makeshift hitch and all, down the narrow path to the fountain. It took both boys to tip the statue over the edge of the fountain and onto the trailer. They hopped in the cart and slowly pulled away, with Eddie riding backwards to keep the statue from sliding and the hitch from popping off. They waited in the shadow of the Lauffers' garage as a neighbor's car pulled out of a driveway on the far side of the cul-de-sac. The trailer hitch threatened to release when they hit the curb to the street, but it held. Eddie could see the relief in Mike's face as soon as they crossed the road and started down the dark path to the golf course. They'd made it!

Mike drove across several fairways and cart trails to get to an unusually thick section of woods. Eddie had no idea where they were headed. He appreciated Mike's thorough knowledge of the course.

"Nobody will ever find this thing back here," Mike said. He backed the trailer to the edge of the thick brush and pushed in until the wheels started to skid. Mike gave one of the mermaid's nipples a final tweak for good luck, and they shoved her off the back of the trailer. The statue flipped once then slid deep into the undergrowth.

"Nicely done, Ghetti. I think we've earned these." Mike reached into the cart's storage compartment and pulled out two extra tall cans of beer. On occasion, Mike and Eddie had liberated a few beers from his father's garage fridge, but none of them had ever tasted this good.

# Chapter 4 - The Third Task: Donuts, Anyone?

Mike Ashland jolted suddenly awake, as though from a dream with a violent end. Bright sunshine filled his room, and he panicked. Why didn't his alarm go off? He recalled he had no school today, and enjoyed a brief moment of relaxation.

He tensed up again, remembering the mermaid theft from last night. Had they really covered their tracks as well as they thought? The whole thing seemed like a crazy idea now. Spray painting a sign could be passed off as a victimless prank, but stealing someone's property clearly crossed the line into criminal activity. Could he afford to risk his future for some quick cash? He mentally reviewed the details. He had returned the tools to the garage, had a plausible "yardwork" excuse for leaving the golf cart and trailer in the yard (if anyone even noticed), and Ghetti had taken care of the empty beer cans. Had they missed anything? Once again, he wondered if they would ever see a dime of the reward money, or if they had just been played for fools.

He stood and looked out his window. From his angle, he couldn't quite see the center of the Lauffers' fountain. Had the old lady noticed? He finished dressing and bounded down the stairs to the kitchen. Next to the sink, his mother stood whipping up her famous pancake batter. He could already smell the bacon, so he decided to postpone any further investigation.

"Morning, Cowboy!" she greeted him. "Ready for some breakfast?"

"Morning, Mom. You bet!" He sat down at their large kitchen table, already adorned with place settings for the whole family. So far, all four of the settings sat untouched.

"Dad's not up yet?"

"In the shower. He's on his way to the club again. More presidential business, I guess."

The way his mother said "presidential business" sounded a bit sarcastic to Mike. For the first time, he thought perhaps his mother resented her husband's extensive involvement with the club. He knew his father spent a considerable amount of time there, but his mother always seemed to enjoy the social status his role as president had earned them. They certainly looked the part; many of their friends referred to them as the "Kennedys in Camelot." Though his parents were both nearly fifty, they kept in great shape and seemed so much younger than their age. To round it off, his mother had established herself as a member of the Sutter Valley School Board. For any community volunteer or fundraising project you could name, Mary Ashland had either organized it herself or was at least directly involved. She always appeared to have boundless energy, enthusiasm and kindness.

As a mother, her generous and cheerful nature had been so ubiquitous that Mike had never imagined her as forlorn, apart from grieving for a friend. He wondered if maybe she no longer enjoyed the presidential lifestyle quite as much. Did he just imagine it?

"You OK, Mom?" he asked.

"I'm fine." She gave him a quizzical look. "How 'bout you?"

"I'm great, Mom. You just sounded kinda bummed out."

"I'm as fine as can be, Champ. Maybe just a little tired." She smiled and loaded Mike's plate with a massive strawberry pancake and three fat slabs of bacon.

Mike choked his breakfast down as fast as he politely could. He thanked his mother and blasted through the sliding door to the back deck. Once outside, he looked across the yards to the scene of the crime. He worried about any telltale tracks from the trailer or golf cart they may have left.

The entire view of the Lauffers' back yard looked different without the mermaid. Though he had never paid much attention to it in the past, her absence now created a noticeable openness around the gardens. The fountain water supply must have turned on. A wide dome of water now boiled where the mermaid had reigned for so many years. How long would it be before Old Lady Lauffer realized?

He could see Eddie strolling over to join him. Knowing Eddie, he had probably waited over an hour for Mike to venture outside.

"Hey, Mike," Eddie casually greeted him. "How's it going?"

"Hey, Ghetti. Doing good. How 'bout you?" Mike thought Eddie sounded somewhat fake and loud, as though someone else might be listening. After walking a few steps closer to Eddie's yard, he realized why. A sheriff's car sat parked in the Lauffers' driveway. Guess the old lady missed her mermaid already. He could feel his body tense up. He promised himself that if they got away with this task, he would do no more.

"Somebody stole the mermaid out of the Lauffers' fountain," Eddie continued in his louder-than-necessary voice while thumbing at the fountain.

Mike couldn't see the sheriff, but he picked up on the cue just in case. He tried to appear astonished as he surveyed the vacant fountain.

"Oh man! Who would've taken it?"

Eddie shrugged and motioned for Mike to walk with him back towards Mike's yard.

Once out of earshot, Eddie nodded towards the hedgerow behind Mike's pool.

"I saw the sheriff look at the golf cart and trailer when he first went back to the fountain."

"Shit," said Mike. "You think he knows? Did he talk to you yet?"

Eddie shook his head.

"Well, we had to leave it out there. If I'd hit the garage door opener that late, it woulda woke up my whole family."

"I know. I don't think he can prove anything, anyway. I'm not even sure he put it all together. Just scared me when he looked right at it."

"Where is he now?"

"I think he's inside with Old Lady Lauffer, probably filling out paperwork."

Mike sighed. "Well, we probably shouldn't let him see us out here staring at the tools of the crime, right?"

"Yeah, good point. Besides, I want to see if the Gamemaster gave us credit for the task yet."

"You didn't check it this morning?"

Eddie shook his head. "I figured we should watch it together. Mostly 'cause this whole thing is kinda freakin' me out."

"I totally get that. I say we collect the bucks from this gig and call it done."

Eddie looked like he was about to argue, then decided against it. He scanned the Lauffer's backyard for the sheriff, then led the way to the shed.

To Mike's relief, no surprises from the Hoodlum laptop. A simple acknowledgement that the task had been verified, and directions to the same reward pickup spot as before. Within minutes they had grabbed their bikes and zipped across the street to the golf course access trail. Eddie had stopped at the top of the trail to look down at the course below.

"Wow – it's another great day," he said. "I can't believe there's hardly anyone playing. It was mobbed yesterday."

"We got the day off from school, but most people still have work," Mike explained. "Even teachers had to go in today."

"Yeah, that's right. I gotta work at the store tonight, too. Makes for an easy reward pickup, though." He flew down the access trail to join the cart path. Mike stole a quick glance at the Lauffer driveway where the sheriff's car remained. For a fleeting second, he envisioned Eddie and himself locked in the back seat, heads hung low while his family and neighbors looked on in shocked disappointment. He turned and followed Eddie to pick up the cash.

---

By the time they'd returned to Eddie's garage, the sheriff had left. Mike had mentally prepared himself for questioning, but was delighted to avoid the situation altogether. They might be questioned again in the future, of course, but for now they were off the hook.

Eddie made a big show out of counting the cash out, looking like a mob boss in a gangster movie. Except for birthday money, which his parents always made him save in his college account, Mike never had this much cash just handed to him *to spend however he wanted.* This would certainly help out on date nights. Now that he had his license, having this much cash available opened the door to some attractive options. And he had to believe this felt like winning the lottery for Eddie. Though he had no idea how much Eddie's mom actually made, he knew it had to be far less than what his father brought home. Eddie had never told him, but he was pretty sure that at least some of Eddie's wages from the grocery store went towards paying the bills. He didn't have to wonder; he knew for certain that Eddie would want to keep playing Hoodlum. The lure of easy cash would just be too much for him to resist. Mike knew he had to shut this down hard and fast.

"I'm glad we got paid, Ghetti," he said, "but I'm out. No more Hoodlum for me."

Eddie looked stunned.

"Come on, man. We've got to at least check out the next task. Just to see what it is. We can still quit after that, if you want."

Mike exhaled dramatically. "I'm sorry, but I'm done, Ghetti. The cop car made it too real for me."

"Look, I was nervous too, but we *did* it, Bro! Two hundred bucks each!" Eddie flapped through his stack of cash like a blackjack dealer. "Let's just check out the next challenge, even if we don't really do it."

Mike knew that Eddie would read the challenge anyway, no matter what he told him. Worse than that, though, he worried that Eddie might secretly plan to do the next challenge himself – risk be damned. Eddie and his mother's financial situation might be all the justification that he needed to strike off on his own.

Even though Eddie was a few months older than him, Mike felt like he owned the role of Eddie's big brother. Beyond Eddie not having a dad, the kid had always struck him as a lost dog, with no one else to look out for him. On more than one occasion Mike had bailed him out of fights with bigger kids and talked him out of bad decisions. He knew that Eddie was a great kid at heart, but this Hoodlum game felt like another bad decision that would require a firm shutdown.

"Ghetti, you know damn well that you'll talk me into it again as soon as we read it. Just like last time. And the time before!"

"Dude, I promise we'll decide together. Go or no go. You know you want to see what it is. Come on, Mike." Eddie beckoned towards the door to the backyard and shed, doing his best Vanna White impersonation.

Mike caved. Part of him really did need to see the next challenge, but he wanted even more to figure out who could possibly be behind this whole weird thing. If they went no further, he may never know.

"Ok, ok," Mike slumped his shoulders and followed Eddie back to the shed. "Let's see what it is. But remember what you promised – we decide together, right? Go or no go."

"I promise. You get the final call." Eddie had the computer out of the bag and powered up before he had even finished promising.

"This one's a thousand bucks!" Eddie exclaimed. His face showed a strange mixture of delight and concern as he read the details of the next challenge. He turned the screen to show Mike. From Eddie's expression, Mike guessed he would not like the task at all. And he was right.

Task three required them to "borrow" a tractor from the golf course maintenance shed, use it to vandalize a specific part of the golf course, then leave clues that would implicate another house in the neighborhood as the home of the vandal. The task did not name the homeowner, just the address. The task also involved picking up some additional "tools for the job," in an envelope where they first found the Hoodlum bag.

Mike vigorously shook his head.

"Ghetti, there's no way in hell that we're doing this. It's the golf course. My father would skin me alive."

"Ok, Ok, I figured that as soon as I saw it. Let's just talk it through."

Mike covered his ears while backing out of the shed.

"No way in hell. And remember your promise. We checked it out, and I'm saying no. You're not doing it either!"

"Mike. Just listen. Let's see who's house the address is. That's gotta be a big clue to figuring out what this is all about. We don't have to do the task; we'll just figure out who they're setting up." He followed Mike back to the garage.

Mike stopped and considered. Checking out the address seemed harmless enough. No crime in that, and Eddie was right. Finding out the intended victim of the frame-up could be an important clue. Once again, his shoulders sagged in defeat. Without waiting for a verbal response, Eddie leaped back on his bike, and they tore off down the street.

Both boys knew the street name of the intended victim well. Several of their classmates lived on the street, but they had no idea what any of their house numbers were. Frontier Lane wound around the far side of the golf course and ended at the entrance to the prestigious Sutter Valley Golf Course clubhouse itself.

Eddie suddenly cut sharply left from the far-right edge of the road, as Mike expected. Every kid in town used the Grassy Trail Loop to shortcut the distance between the local streets. Cars had to follow the perimeter road that circled around the entire golf course to get from one street to the next. But bikers, walkers, and even moms with strollers used the Grassy Trail Loop to move through the neighborhood. The greenskeepers hated the fact that this unofficial trail cut through the golf course quite unattractively. Years ago, they had tried to shut it down with signs and rope barriers. Enforcing the shutdown against so many offenders proved impossible, however, so the greenskeepers turned a blind eye to the garish scar across their beloved course. The latest real estate brochure for the neighborhood even included the trail on the inset map.

Less than five minutes later, Eddie and Mike emerged at another residential street on the opposite end of the Grassy Trail Loop. Eddie paused to figure out which direction the addresses were going, then turned left to continue down Frontier Lane. Mike's curiosity piqued as they pressed on. He recognized the homes of several friends as they rode by. Who could it possibly be?

"Must be close to the Clubhouse," Eddie yelled back to Mike.

Sure enough, the address 5032 sat only three houses away from the entranceway to the Sutter Valley Golf Course clubhouse. With the exception of the Lauffers' place, the homes near the entrance of the clubhouse were the largest and most beautiful in the development.

Mike had already recognized the home before even reading the name on the mailbox. The St. Vincent family lived there. Mike had attended soccer team parties at the house several times over the years. Geoff St. Vincent had played soccer on

Mike's team since middle school. Mike thought Geoff played OK as a goalie, but he tried too hard to act like a tough guy. Though Mike did not consider him a friend, they had always gotten along well enough. That is, right up until two weeks ago.

Mike had walked into the team locker room to hear Geoff bragging about some "serious action" he got from some hot freshman girl. When Geoff saw Mike, he sniggered and whispered to the others, "Don't tell Mikey, though!"

The other boys had laughed, but stopped when they saw Mike's reaction.

"Who're you talking about, Geoff? You got something to say to me? Who're you talking about?" He couldn't imagine that his girlfriend, Beth, would have anything to do with this pudgy jackass. Then it hit him that Geoff was talking about a freshman. His sister, Cindy!

Geoff laughed again as Mike came to the realization. "I'm sure she's a nice girl at home, though."

Without thinking, Mike slammed Geoff into the lockers behind him. Before either boy had even thrown a punch, their teammates had intervened. Things had settled down before the coach came in, but he and Geoff had only exchanged burning glares since the incident. When he'd asked Cindy about Geoff at home, she had denied ever even talking to him.

"Do you know whose house this is?" Eddie had stopped at the mailbox.

"Yeah. St. Vincent's." Mike scowled.

"The dipshit that says he's dating Cindy?"

"Yeah. She hasn't even talked to him, but he's talking all kinds of shit about what they did together." Mike could feel his face redden. "She's not dating anyone."

"What a douche!" Eddie suddenly looked even madder than Mike. "We gotta do this challenge now. It's not even about the money. It's for Cindy!"

Mike felt a wave of realization suddenly flow over him. Could Eddie be the Gamemaster after all? He had everything to gain by making Mike's dad hate Geoff. The whole Ashland family knew about Eddie's crush on Cindy. They teased her about it when Eddie wasn't around, but Mike never let on to Eddie that they all knew. It still didn't make sense, though. He didn't doubt that Eddie could program the computer to do this stuff; the kid was brilliant. He also came up with the strategies to accomplish each task very quickly. Almost like he had prior knowledge. But how could he possibly afford the cash rewards? Had he saved his grocery store job money for this? Mike just couldn't believe it. Crush or not. And if Eddie was the Gamemaster, his acting performance was worthy of an academy award. His reactions to the tasks, the rewards and everything else seemed too real to be anything but genuine.

"Hold on, Ghetti. No matter how much we hate this jackass, this is some serious shit. We could've passed the sign and even the mermaid thing off as stupid pranks, but this one is a lot more serious. For one thing, I don't want to rip the crap out of the golf course 'cuz of my dad, but I don't want to get caught trying to frame someone else for the crime, either. This seems a lot worse to me than the last one. A *lot* worse."

"But think about it," Eddie argued. "The golf course damage won't be a big deal. Those golf course workers are usually bored out of their skull. You've seen 'em hanging out behind the garage and the clubhouse, just smoking for hours. This'd give 'em something to do!" Eddie thumbed towards the St. Vincent home. "And this bastard has it coming. If we don't do this, it's like he'll never pay for what he said about Cindy. People will just believe him, even though it isn't true. And there's nothing we can do about it."

Mike shook his head. "We came up here to check out the address, just to see if it gave us any idea who the Gamekeeper really is. And we still don't know."

"Gamemaster. And at least we know it isn't Geoff. Gotta be someone who doesn't like him or Old Lady Lauffer. Or the golf course." Eddie's eyes widened. "Maybe it's Cindy!"

Mike laughed at the thought. "That would be the prank of the year. But I don't think she hates the golf course, or Old Lady Lauffer." He tried to remember if he'd ever even seen Cindy use a computer outside of watching idiotic YouTube videos. She earned somewhat decent grades at school, but certainly didn't possess the ability to set up the Hoodlum game.

"Let's check out the 'special tools' for the challenge, too. That might be another clue about the Gamemaster. Come on, Mike. That's not a crime."

"Sure Ghetti. What the hell."

The boys circled the bikes and rode back to Eddie's house to drop them off. They jogged down to the pond and retrieved a manila envelope tucked into the same clump of grass. Eddie tore it open.

Inside was a printed index card, a keychain with a single key, and Geoff St. Vincent's student ID card. Eddie flipped the bird at Geoff's grinning mug on the ID and read the note aloud.

"Bolt cutters will be leaning against the left side of the shed for the padlock. Key is for the tractor. Leave the tractor at the damage site when finished. Leave ID card next to tractor. Leave bolt cutters at the shed. Leave tractor key and broken padlock hidden in the front porch landscaping of the address listed in the task instructions."

Eddy flipped the instructions so Mike could see for himself. He noted with some amusement that even though the index card was printed, the author had used the "ransom note" font to make it look like the letters were cut out from magazines, like ransom notes in the movies. You had to give the Gamemaster credit for attention to detail.

"Well, it must be someone that could get the tractor key, or at least get a copy made."

"Yeah," said Eddie. "Maybe a disgruntled greenskeeper, with ace-level computer skills? That would explain his easy access to the tractor shed and the pond down here. And even the reward payoff drops at the hole four tee. But what would he have against Geoff, or Old Lady Lauffer? And how would he get Geoff's ID?"

"Maybe one or more of those things is just to throw us off track. Or maybe the next task will piss off even more random people, and there is no real overall motive. Who knows?"

"Five hundred bucks each, Mike. And revenge for your sister's honor. I say we do this. I think it'll even be fun!"

Mike waggled his head in reluctant consent. "When?"

"I got work every night this week but Thursday. How 'bout then? Will you be able to sneak out on a school night?"

"Yeah. I can get out the bathroom window and drop off the front porch. Getting out is easy; getting back in is the tricky part."

Mike started the uphill walk back to his house. A small part of his conscience felt bad for setting up Geoff to take the fall for a crime he didn't commit, but he agreed with Eddie. The lying bastard did deserve something like this for what he'd been saying about Cindy. At this point, he no longer thought this could be a reality show or video prank gimmick. That would have been bad enough. Mike's biggest concern was that he had no idea what this was all about, and it could all blow wide open if anything went wrong. He patted the pocket with his recently earned cash, trying to calm his knotted stomach.

How did he get roped into doing this again?

---

The next few days at school passed by uneventfully. Most kids had seen the 80 MPH speed limit sign, but no one had heard about the mermaid theft - at least no one that Mike talked to. He ran into Eddie on Thursday, who seemed disappointed that their crimes hadn't made a bigger public splash. Mike spotted him by his locker between classes. He grabbed his arm, and they slipped out of the mainstream hallway traffic into a vacant classroom to talk.

"I can't believe that more people aren't talking about this stuff," Eddie said.

"Totally fine with me. I'd rather not have everyone on a witch hunt for vandals 'til we get through this."

"Yeah, you're right. I'm just surprised. I thought the speed limit thing would at least get some laughs. Did you run into your buddy Geoff yet?"

"He's in my English and Math classes. We just kinda ignore each other."

"Any other thoughts about who could be doing this?" Eddie asked.

Mike shook his head. "I've been thinking about it a lot, but I got nothing. There're a few guys that don't like him much, and I'm sure a few girls, too. But no one that could set all this up. You sure it ain't you?" He passed the question off as if joking, but in truth he wanted to carefully study Eddie's reaction.

Eddie tilted his head, reminding Mike of a confused dog. He looked as though he couldn't tell if Mike wanted an answer or not.

"Dude, I swear on my left nut it ain't me. I don't have the cash to pay these rewards, and I wouldn't have paid that much to get rid of Lauffer's mermaid, even if I did. And I hope you know I'd never make you trash your dad's golf course. Use your head, Bro."

Mike hadn't considered that. Eddie wouldn't do something like that to their family. They had practically grown up as brothers. Even if he did want Geoff out of his way to get to Cindy, he wouldn't do anything so purposefully hurtful to his father, nor to Mike.

"I believe you, man. It's just driving me crazy."

"Me too. We'll figure it out."

"Yeah. Hopefully not from our jail cells. See you at 8:30?"

Eddie fist-bumped him and merged back into the flowing river of students.

---

Hours later, Mike quietly closed the second-floor bathroom window from the porch roof. Both of his parents had turned in early for once, and he could see no light at all under their bedroom door. Same story with Cindy's room. Sweet. He'd chosen a black sweatshirt, black jeans and his dark blue track shoes for tonight's mission.

The two story drop from his own bedroom window into the back yard was out of the question, and his father had the downstairs rigged with an alarm system that he ran from his phone. That left the upstairs bathroom window as the only reasonable option for sneaking in and out undetected.

He crab-walked down the porch roof to the side near Eddie's house. Looking over the edge into empty blackness, it occurred to him that he had never made this drop in the dark. Hoping to hell that no one had moved something painful below him, he twisted and pushed off at the same time. On landing, he rolled on his side to minimize the impact of the drop. As he stood, he saw a dark figure lurking next to the house, only ten feet away.

"Jesus, Ghetti! You scared the crap out of me!"

He could see Eddies toothy grin, even in the darkness. "I got the key and the card. Let's go!"

They had already decided not to take their bikes. If someone approached while they were on the tractor, they could duck into the woods and make their way back home on foot. Bringing the bikes would mean they'd have to double back to pick them up, risking detection and capture. Besides, the walk to the tractor shed would take only a few minutes. Eddie had left his bike next to his own shed, however, so he could drop off the padlock and tractor key when they'd finished with the tractor.

Mike noticed how dark the night had already turned. Not as much cloud cover tonight, but the tall trees surrounding the fairways blocked most of the exposing moonlight. They walked in silence to the large unlit shed at the edge of the hole six fairway. Eddie searched around the shed to see if there was any kind of wiring box for an alarm system or cameras. He couldn't find anything; not even lines for electrical power.

As promised, the bolt cutters stood leaning against the wooded side of the shed -- invisible to anyone casually walking by the front. Eddie grabbed them and tried to cut the shaft of the padlock, but he couldn't quite close the handles. Mike gave him an assist, and the severed padlock thudded to the ground. Eddie pointed to a paint-on label on the bolt cutters. Mike shined his mag light on the label, revealing the name "St. Vincent."

"Guess we don't need to worry about fingerprints," Eddie laughed.

Mike tossed the cutters into the brush along the side of shed. Just enough to look as though the intruder had attempted to conceal them but had been careless. Eddie picked up the padlock and stuffed it in his pocket for later.

They had to drag an enormous mower deck out of the way, but that gave them plenty of room between the tractor and the door. Mike stuck the key in the ignition but had to search to find the choke and starter. Eddie perched himself above the rear axle, standing behind the seat to help Mike look. He eventually figured out that the starter was an unlabeled button above the ignition switch, and the tractor roared to life. The controls seemed otherwise intuitive. They killed their flashlights as Mike backed the tractor out onto the fairway.

As they rolled towards the green for hole six, Mike felt an unsettling sensation in his stomach. He recognized its cause immediately. Despite what Eddie had said about feeling no guilt for damaging the course, Mike felt terrible about it. While he knew that the damage could be fixed, he shared his father's pride in how beautiful the course looked. He had played here countless times with his parents and knew every fairway and green by heart. This green in particular could be seen from the clubhouse deck, and the view of the various bunkers and water hazards for several of the surrounding holes had been captured in a stunning photo displayed in the clubhouse lobby. He could not help but imagine how his father would feel when he looked down and saw the damage inflicted on his perfectly manicured kingdom. Worse yet, he pictured his reaction if he learned that his own son was responsible. He dismissed those thoughts with visions of Geoff's smirking fat face, bragging about groping his sister, and pressed on.

Once on the green, he told Eddie to jump off. The challenge required at least four complete donuts on the green. This would take less than a minute on the ATV, but he had no idea if the back end of the tractor would slide well enough on the dry green. His first two attempts failed miserably, and he nearly rolled the tractor off the edge of the green. He hoped to God that no one had heard the noise they must be making. But they'd already taken the tractor. No going back now...

With Eddie cheering him on, he shifted to the highest gear, stood on the footbrake, turned the wheel hard left and gunned it. As soon as he released the brake, the tractor whipped around in a tight circle, tearing up the green and slinging grass and dirt everywhere. After three full spins, he regained traction and had to repeat the procedure for one more circle. He shut it down and leapt off the tractor, careful not to get any mud on his clothes. Eddie jogged over and dropped the ID card on the muddy ground near the tractor seat. He grabbed the tractor key to plant at Geoff's along with the padlock.

Eddie looked delighted, but Mike could only muster a half-hearted high five in return. He took a final look back at the green. Even in the darkness he could tell the green had been devastated. His stomach clenched hard. He felt like throwing up for the entire walk home.

Eddie must have sensed his regret and gave him a supportive pat on the back. "Five hundred bucks, Mike. And for Cindy. You should feel proud."

"I dunno, Ghetti. This one didn't feel like the other times. I'm gonna pass on the beers tonight, OK?"

"That's cool. It's already getting late. You gonna be able to get back on your roof?"

"Yeah." Mike fist bumped Eddie and climbed up on the porch railing. The transition from rail to roof proved challenging, but he made it. As he laid flat along the edge of the roof catching his breath, he watched Eddie take off on his bike to plant the evidence at the St. Vincent's.

Part of him envied Eddie's lack of parental supervision. He could pretty much come and go as he pleased. An even bigger part of him envied the fact that Eddie didn't have to worry about his father's reaction to the vandalism when he got home from school tomorrow.

## Chapter 5 - Repercussions

Eddie couldn't wait for school to be over, but they hadn't even gone to lunch yet. He didn't check the Hoodlum computer before school. They wouldn't have had time to grab the reward yet anyway, even if the Gamemaster had already confirmed the task.

He knew it had crushed Mike to vandalize his father's golf course, and he would probably want to quit playing the game. If he planned to include Mike in any more of the tasks, he would need to do some serious convincing. He hoped Mike's adventurous spirit would reawaken when they each held five hundred bucks in their hands. Also, an idea for discovering the identity of the Gamemaster had occurred to him. Maybe this new "unofficial" challenge of their own would be enough to keep Mike engaged.

Had their latest task been noticed yet? The autumn air felt a little cool, but the conditions looked otherwise fantastic through his classroom windows. Any retired golfers taking advantage of the weather must have encountered the damaged green by now. And the missing tractor may have been reported by the morning greens crew even earlier. How long before they discovered the labeled bolt cutters and ID card?

He wished he could see Geoff's face when they confronted him with the evidence. Long before his recent involvement with Cindy, Geoff had been part of the group of jocks that had picked on Eddie over the years. They hadn't really physically hassled him – Mike had seen to that. But they still made fun of him in Phys Ed class whenever they picked teams or "accidentally" knocked books out of his hands in the hallways. Yes, a little revenge seemed long overdue.

And he was thrilled to hear Mike say that Cindy wasn't dating *anyone*. He didn't feel quite ready to ask her out himself, but at least she had not been removed from the realm of possibility. A glimmer of hope remained.

These thoughts drifted through his mind, much more engrossing than the advanced English lesson that he should have been listening to. He swept his eyes around the classroom. A few jocks in this class, but they were seniors. Eddie and a few other kids in their class had moved ahead a full year in several classes. He knew Mike was much brighter than these guys, but he wasn't focused enough on his grades to move ahead.

The classroom also included a number of pretty girls, but none that would ever consider him boyfriend material. And that was fine with Eddie. To him, their conversations seemed so superficial and mindless. A few of them seemed outright obnoxious to the teacher and everyone else, and no amount of beauty could compensate for that.

He did like Emma, a friendly girl that often laughed at his occasional soft-spoken comments. When called upon in class, her contributions were always intelligent and insightful. Eddie estimated that she was probably brighter than all of the "snobby" girls in the class combined. Though no beauty queen, Eddie thought she had a kind face and infectious smile. He sensed that she didn't quite fit in with the popular girls, but had made her own peace with the situation. She must have felt his gaze; she suddenly looked his way and flashed a quick smile. He smiled back, but she had already turned away.

Thinking about Emma allowed his mind to drift even further away from the lecture. He wondered about the nature of true love. Or more precisely, that initial spark of attraction that often *led* to true love. For guys, it seemed their individual perception of physical beauty was that primary spark. He knew physical attraction was the key factor for his infatuation with Cindy. When he thought about it, he realized he didn't really know her as a person at all despite living next door to her for all these years. He didn't think she was like the snobby girls in this class, though. At least not yet.

He imagined physical attraction held true for girls' interest in guys as well, but there were other "compensating factors" like wealth, power, talent, or, hopefully – intelligence. But if that were really the case, did that mean that everyone only *truly* desired those favored unattainable few, and most people just "settled" for someone that roughly matched their corresponding position on the attractiveness scale? The thought seemed very un-romantic, like a mathematical assignment of a mate. The unfairness of it saddened him.

He tried to imagine himself as Emma's boyfriend. He pictured her as very loving, supportive and devoted. He knew he would really like Emma, but could he grow to truly love her, the way he thought he loved Cindy now? Was he confusing love with lust? Emma seemed like a sweet girl, certainly worthy of someone's genuine love. The whole love situation seemed like a torturously cruel imbalance. Bottom line – even with Geoff out of the picture, he just couldn't bring himself to ask Cindy out.

At last the class ended, and he scurried along with the rest of the bustling herd to the cafeteria. Mike's lunch period was just ending, so he stopped by his locker to see if he'd heard anything. To Eddie, he looked terrible. As though he hadn't slept in days.

"Any news from the club?" he asked.

"My mother texted me about it. She said dad's really upset and took it very personally. That course means everything to him." Mike sighed heavily.

"Sorry, Bro. Hopefully he'll get over it quick."

"Maybe," Mike said, but didn't sound like he thought that was very likely at all.

"Did they say anything about suspects?" Eddie whispered.

Mike just shook his head. "Nothing yet. I'll talk to you in the shed later, OK?"

Eddie nodded and continued to lunch. In all the years he'd known him, he had never seen Mike this upset. He worried that even his new idea to catch the Gamemaster would not be enough to keep him in the game.

---

Back in Eddie's garage after school, Mike didn't look any better. It had started to rain, so Eddie had pulled the bucket with the laptop into the garage. He opened it while Mike gave the report from his father.

"He came home early, and he's still totally pissed," Mike said. "They found the ID card and bolt cutters, but Geoff is denying the whole thing."

"No surprise there," Eddie said. "Even if he did do it, he would never admit it."

"Yeah, well here's the problem. He's got an alibi. He and Tom Blackmoore were at some country music concert last night and didn't get home 'til like two in the morning."

"He could be making that up. For all they know, Tom could've been in on it, too."

"Thought of that. Guess what? Tom's father Roddy, our friendly neighborhood state cop, was with them the whole time. How do ya like that for an alibi?" Mike kicked the metal pole in the middle of the garage. "Ya know, busting that douchebag Geoff was the only reason I even did this. I don't give a shit about the money."

"But they still could've done it when they got back, right? They don't know when the damage was done."

"My father says the alibi is airtight. His secretary is the cop's wife, and they're all saying it's an obvious frame-up. The St. Vincents even came forward themselves with the busted lock and tractor key you planted."

"Shit. Did your dad say they had any ideas about who might have framed him?"

"He didn't tell me, but I'm sure I'll be high on Geoff's list of possible enemies that he'll give them. If he hasn't already." Mike grabbed his head in his hands, as though it would just be a matter of time before he got busted.

"Dude, beside the fact that your dad is the club president, everyone knows you're the nicest guy in the school. You're literally the last person they'd ever suspect."

"I sure hope so, Ghetti. I'd like to friggin' strangle that bastard, but right now I can't even risk looking at him."

"I know, man. We'll get him somehow. Not right away, but we'll get him. In the meantime, let's see about collecting our reward."

Eddie had already powered up the laptop while they were talking. Before sharing his new plan with Mike, he wanted to be certain he was right. Sure enough, the screen not only confirmed the task completion, but told them to pick up the reward at the same location: the hole four tee.

"Yes!" Eddie shouted, startling Mike. "Same pickup place!"

"What?" Mike asked. "Is there something else about Geoff?"

"No. But I figured out a way to catch the Gamemaster. Should've thought of it sooner."

"How?"

"The Gamemaster always uses the same spot for dropping off the reward cash. If we can borrow your dad's trail camera, we can catch him when he plants the cash!"

"What if he pays someone else to plant it for him?"

"As long as it's someone we recognize, we can either follow them around until they meet up with the real Gamemaster, or just pay them to tell us who it is."

Mike nodded, then exhaled dramatically. Eddie could tell he was preparing to make a speech.

"Ghetti, I'll get his camera for you, if I can find it, but I'm out. For real, this time. I don't want to hear the next challenge, or even look at that goddam laptop again. The reward money for the last task is all yours, too."

"No way, man. I couldn't have done any of these things alone, especially the tractor one. You gotta take your money."

"Not one dime, Ghetti. I'm serious." Mike looked at him gravely. "I know you're probably going to keep going with this, but I gotta tell you a few things, OK?"

"Sure, Mike. What?"

"First of all, you know whoever is doing this knows exactly who we are. Remember how and where you found the bag, right? There's no way in hell that it was meant for anyone but us."

Eddie nodded.

"So, I have no idea what this Hoodlum game is all about, but I do know that people don't just give big money away for stupid shit like this without having a good reason. I'm worried that they're setting us up to take the fall for something really huge. And this is the worst possible time in our lives for either of us to get busted. You're the smartest kid I know, Ghetti, and you've got a great shot at going to a good college. Or the military, if that's really what you want. But I worry about your judgment sometimes, especially when it comes to money. I'm afraid that you're going to blow your whole future chasing after a few bucks playing this crazy fucking game."

Eddie nodded again and started to speak, but Mike silenced him with a wave of his hand.

"I'm not done. While I was sweating out our latest little project, another fun thought occurred to me. You know how you're planning to capture the Gamemaster on camera? What if he's already done that to us?"

That was something Eddie had not considered.

"If he has," Mike continued, "he won't even need to offer cash to make you do these crimes. He can just blackmail you to do one crime after another, using the video from your last crime to threaten you for the next one. Think about it, Ghetti. By Christmas, you'll probably be killing people."

Eddie snorted, but then realized that Mike was dead serious.

"You're right. I gotta check out the next challenge, though. I promise I won't do it if it's too risky. And the money is important to me, but so is figuring out who is behind all this. I can't even think about anything else."

Mike shrugged and continued.

"So, I want you to keep my share of the money for the last one, but I have a request. I hope to God that you stop playing Hoodlum, but I'm pretty sure you won't. Even if you tell me you're quitting. Here's what I'm asking: If you do get caught going out on your own, can you please keep my name out of it?"

Eddie felt relieved that this was Mike's request. He had worried that Mike was going to take the laptop or destroy it. At the very least, he did not expect Mike to let him out of his original promise not to go it alone.

"Of course, Bro. I wouldn't rat you out. You don't need to pay me for that. We've been friends for too long."

"Keep it, Ghetti. I didn't really think you'd sell me out. I just don't want the money. After seeing how bummed out my dad is, I'd feel like shit taking any amount of money for what I did to him."

Eddie nodded once again. "I get that. I feel bad about that part of it too. And for talking you into it."

"It was my decision. I'm a big boy, and I knew the risk. But now I'm out. And I hope you will be too, Ghetti. Are we good?"

Mike stood to leave.

"We're good, Mike. And I promise I'll be careful."

He wanted to remind him about the trail camera but decided to let it go for now. The rain outside had really picked up. He watched Mike dodge his way around the puddles back to his house.

His warnings really did have Eddie concerned, especially the possibility that the Gamemaster had taken video of them doing any of these crimes. The Hoodlum game could just be a ruse to set them up for something really serious. The more he thought about it, the more it made sense. But what could he do? If he quit the game now, would the blackmail videos start to appear in his e-mail? Maybe it was already too late to quit. Then it occurred to him that his plan to catch the Gamemaster just might be his only way out. If the Hoodlum game did turn into blackmail missions, he could counter by threatening to expose the Gamemaster's identity and the whole Hoodlum scheme.

In any case, he knew he would need to see the next challenge. If he decided it was going to be too risky, he could just wait and see what happened next.

As always, he could think of little else besides the next task. If he wanted to find out before work, that meant picking up the reward right away -- in the pouring rain. On top of that, he would need to grab dinner early tonight so he'd have enough time to get to work by 6:30.

---

Absolutely no one on the course, so Eddie coasted right up to the hole four tee and snagged the envelope. He didn't notice any increased security, which he took as a good sign.

The Gamemaster must have anticipated the bad weather; the envelope was inside a waterproof courier sleeve. Nice touch. That made him feel a bit more trusting of the Gamemaster since his conversation with Mike.

He took a moment to look around for potential trail camera locations. On the opposite side of the tee from the ball washer stood a fairly dense cluster of undergrowth and small trees. That was the only spot close enough to get a good enough picture. He'd seen pictures from the camera before, and the quality was far from good. Mike's father used it before deer season every year to select hunting spots where big bucks were likely to frequent. Over the years he had shared pictures of deer, coyotes, and even a mother black bear with a cub that the camera had captured.

Though the picture quality was poor, the trail camera was triggered by motion. It only took pictures when something was moving in the camera's field of view. Of course there would be a number of nuisance golfer pics, but this would be much better than having to scan through endless hours of video. Besides, he didn't have a video camera.

At some point he would need to place the trail camera before completing the next task. Even if he had already gotten the camera from Mike, he couldn't have planted it now anyway. The Gamemaster would be watching for him to collect the reward, so he could enable the next task.

He biked back to his garage through the rain. The cash was all there. A thousand bucks, all his! For the first time, he worried about hiding the money. Until now, he had stashed his share of the reward cash in an old ammo box that he kept in his bedroom closet. He'd gotten the box at a neighborhood garage sale years ago. Along with the cash, the box held a few old photos, Air Force and Navy recruitment brochures, a wristwatch that didn't work but seemed too expensive to throw away, leftover bottle rockets and an arrowhead he had picked up on a Boy Scout camping trip. He didn't think his mother would ever snoop through the box, but what if she did?

He had never hidden money from his mother. He could tell it bothered her that he had to contribute part of his grocery store paycheck to help pay their bills, but to Eddie it was a source of pride. None of his classmates shared this much responsibility with their parents, as far as he knew.

When he did want to buy something for himself, which wasn't too often, he would ask his mother directly. They would have very frank discussions about what they could and could not afford. She had always been generous; often going without so Eddie could get a bike, decent clothes and other things most neighborhood kids took for granted. In all that time, he had never once felt the need to hide money from her.

But now things were different. If she did find this huge amount of cash, she would suspect him of stealing or dealing drugs. And how could he argue? She would be furious if she knew how he had actually earned it. He wished there was a way he could somehow sneak at least some of this money into their shared bank account. But that seemed even riskier than hiding the cash in his room. She watched the account carefully and would certainly notice any sudden unexplained deposits. And if he opened his own account, the bank would mail statements to their house that she would eventually intercept.

He would have to come up with something better than his ammo box. For now, he shoved the envelope into the laptop bag. He powered up the laptop, but the "Next Task" button was still greyed out. The Gamemaster must not have noticed he had picked up the reward. Dammit! He would have to wait until after work to check again.

He stuffed the laptop in the bag with the cash, slid the bag back in the bucket, and carried it outside to the shed.

## Chapter 6 - The Fourth Task: Incriminating Evidence

"Hey Eddie Bear — I got Chinese!" Tina called from the front door, her arms laden with multiple bags and her purse.

"Awesome!" Eddie shouted from the kitchen. He still hadn't decided what to make for dinner, and was already running short on time. He sprinted down the hall to help his mother bring it in. When he got to the door, he could see the rain had picked up.

"How was your day?" he asked, relieving her of two bags. "I thought you'd be going out tonight."

"Rita had to cancel at the last minute and Cathy is still on vacation. Deb and I just decided to bag it and spend time with our lucky families." She gave Eddie's cheek a playful pinch.

"That's great for dinner, Mom, but I got work at 6:30."

"Bummer. Well at least now you can take the car, so you don't have to ride your bike in the rain."

Eddie set the table in seconds while Tina unpacked the food. Eddie knew the contents of the bags without asking: kung pao shrimp for him, spicy chicken for her, wonton soup and fried rice to share, two egg rolls and two fortune cookies. They shared Chinese food at least once a week, and neither of them ever wavered on their favorites.

During the meal they chatted about work and school. As usual, his mother tried to get Eddie to talk about any "special girls" he liked in his classes, but he politely deflected her questions. As Tina finished eating, she opened her fortune cookie and read it aloud.

"Here's a good one for today. 'If you want the rainbow, you must endure the rain.' Not bad. What did you get?"

Eddie opened his and read. "The betrayal of a close friend is the most selfish crime of all."

Tina squinted. "Nah – I don't think either of these are fridge-worthy." She stood and started to collect the plates and boxes. "I'll clean up. You better get rolling if you need to be there by 6:30." She pulled the keys out of her purse and tossed them to Eddie.

Eddie hugged her goodbye and headed out the door.

---

Eddie had to set the windshield wipers at their highest setting, to what his mother called "spaz mode." The rain pounded down. He felt grateful to her for letting him take the car. He would have been soaked to the bone if he'd ridden his bike.

Though he drove conservatively, he was a confident driver. He loved the sense of control and responsibility. If he could figure out how to launder his growing stash of reward money, he could think about buying a car or maybe a motorcycle of his own. The motorcycle would be cheaper, but he knew his mom would push back hard on that plan.

At the Sutter Valley entrance, he tried to see if his speed limit artwork still remained. He had to look backwards to see it, though, and the dense rain blocked his view anyway.

Silver's Grocery sat less than a mile down the road outside their neighborhood. Though not a big chain grocery store, it was definitely bigger than a "Quickie Mart." Silvers had prospered due to its proximity to the Sutter Valley development. Everyone appreciated the convenience and local charm of the store, and most of the employees were classmates of Eddie's at Sutter Valley High.

Eddie had started working there as soon as he was old enough. Because he learned quickly, treated customers politely and had proven himself reliable, he became one of the only employees who could stock shelves, work the deli counter, bag groceries and run a cash register. That versatility allowed him to work as many shifts as he wanted.

"Nice weather, eh Eddie? We thought you'd probably arrive by boat." Eric Silver, the owner and manager greeted him as he entered.

Eddie always appreciated Eric's sense of humor. Eric had to be about ten years older than his mother, but Eddie secretly thought they would make a great couple. They knew each other only through her shopping trips, though, and Eddie hadn't yet figured out a way to move their friendship beyond that.

"Yeah, it's really coming down! I brought a life preserver for the ride home." he answered.

He hoped the bad weather would discourage most people from coming out to shop tonight. The long week and lack of sleep had taken their toll, and he didn't want to bust his ass working hard for the next few hours. More than anything, he wanted to get back home and find out about the next task.

"Hey Eddie. You on register tonight?" Steve Kagasimi asked.

"Yeah. You too?"

"Yeah. From now 'til closing."

Steve was Eddie's best friend at work. Though not as close of a friend as Mike, Steve shared several advanced classes with Eddie. His father worked as an engineer, and his mother taught mathematics at the local college. Steve and his parents had gotten Eddie involved with Boy Scouts years ago, and they had been long standing lab partners. They had slept over at each other's houses dozens of times when they were younger. The Kagasimi's house was much more fun than his own. They had a cool entertainment center and gaming system, along with tons of sci-fi movies on DVDs. And when it came to playing video games, Steve had no equal.

Eddie had briefly considered Steve as a possible Gamemaster suspect. He certainly had the skills, but he was even more uptight than Mike when it came to breaking rules. His parents were ultra-strict and very much involved in his future college plans. There was just no way Steve Kagasimi would involve himself with anything like Hoodlum.

Eric had been talking to the stock boys, and now joined Steve and Eddie.

"Boys, thanks to this rain it looks like it's going to be a pretty quiet night. You're both welcome to stay if you'd like, or one of you can go home. You'll still get credit on the time clock for an hour. I'll leave it to you to figure out who, OK?"

"I'm fine with staying," Steve offered. "My father wasn't planning to pick me up until after ten anyway."

"Thanks, Steve. I could really use the night off." Eddie had his raincoat on and was back in the car in a flash.

---

The rain had let up a little by the time Eddie got back home, but he still got soaked walking back to the shed. He banged the keyboard through the startup routine. Yes! The Gamemaster had acknowledged the reward pickup, and the new task was available to view.

The fourth task directed him first to pick up another package at the fishing spot. The laptop message went on to mention that the attempt to frame the victim identified in the previous task had failed. The Gamemaster took full responsibility for the blunder, admitting the challenge itself had been performed to the letter. For some reason, the game still didn't use Geoff's name explicitly, even though the previous task "accessories" had included his personal school ID card. Couldn't get much more specific than that.

According to the Gamemaster, this next task would correct the mistake from the previous task. Frustratingly though, no specifics. He couldn't imagine how another task could possibly "fix" the failed frame-up. Additional fake evidence maybe, or something to discredit the concert alibi? Another entirely new crime? The game promised fifteen hundred dollars as the reward for successful completion.

Hopefully the package would offer more detailed information. He really didn't feel like walking down to the fishing spot at night in the rain, and he also worried that his mother had heard the car arrive. She probably hadn't gone to bed yet and would wonder what the hell he was doing outside in the rain for so long. But he just couldn't stand not knowing -- he had to check it out.

The trip down to the fishing hole turned out to be even wetter and muddier than he had imagined. Though he never fell on the slippery ground, it seemed like every wet branch in the forest whapped him in the face on his way to the pickup spot. Cold water seeped down his neck and drenched his work shirt.

He found the package right away, using the mini-LED light from his mother's keychain. Once again, the Gamemaster had taken the nasty weather into account – the manila envelope was sealed within a larger waterproof shipping envelope. He grabbed it and started the wet slog back home.

Because her bedroom light was off, Eddie couldn't tell if his mother was already asleep or still downstairs waiting for him. He decided to sneak the package inside under his coat rather than linger outside even longer to read it in the privacy of the shed. He opened the door from the garage and stepped inside. To his relief, the television was already off along with the upstairs lights. She had left the kitchen and front hallway lights on for him. Must have gone to bed early. He tucked the keys back in her purse and opened the package. The envelope contained only two items; a USB thumb drive and a page of written instructions. He read through the instructions, hoping they might describe how Geoff would again be blamed for trashing the golf course.

For the first time since starting to play, Eddie almost decided to quit the game on the spot. The instructions did not describe the specific contents of the USB drive. They did, however, direct him to temporarily install the thumb drive on *Mike's father's laptop* and power it up. The game warned him not to try to load the thumb drive on any other computer, neither before nor after loading it on Andrew Ashland's PC. For what it was worth, the instructions did reiterate the task information from the Hoodlum laptop, claiming this challenge would "fix" the problem caused by the unfortunate alibi.

Eddie could never even think of doing any wrong to the Ashlands. Having no other living relatives, Eddie and his mother considered them family. Over the years, the Ashlands had helped Eddie and his mother out of countless jams; emergency rides to or from school, car problems, home repairs and the like. He could not imagine the shame he would feel if any of the Ashlands learned he had risked compromising Andrew's work computer for his own financial gain.

Eddie sat on the couch in front of the TV without turning it on. Was this it? Was this the end of his involvement with Hoodlum? He had earned some damn good money, but he could be leaving a great deal more on the table if he walked away. Worse yet, he still had no clue about the identity of the Gamemaster or what was really behind all of this. If he could plant the camera as he planned, this could be the task where he finally out-gamed the Gamemaster!

As he thought of that, he remembered Mike's last warning. If they had been videotaped doing any of these crimes, the Gamemaster wouldn't even need to offer rewards anymore. What if the USB drive included a video of Mike and him trashing the golf course or stealing the Lauffers' mermaid? Could that be what the task meant about "fixing" the alibi problem? Exposing the true culprits in all of these Hoodlum crimes?

After driving himself crazy with different scenarios, he realized he would have to break the rules. He could not risk loading the thumb drive onto Andrew's PC without knowing what was on it. And if the Gamemaster busted him checking it out, so be it. He would walk away and hope to God he didn't get a blackmail message forcing him to do the next task.

He woke their old desktop PC from sleep mode and plugged in the USB stick. To his surprise, the familiar Hoodlum startup screen appeared. After a few seconds another screen showed a flashing red skull at the top. Below the skull, a message in large text:

**WARNING, HOODLUM! YOU WERE INSTRUCTED TO ONLY CONNECT THIS USB TO THE COMPTER IDENTIFIED IN THE TASK INSTRUCTIONS! YOUR CURIOSITY IS UNDERSTANDABLE, BUT YOU MUST TRUST THE GAMEMASTER AND FOLLOW THE INSTRUCTIONS TO THE LETTER!**

**AT POWER UP, AN EXECUTABLE FILE WILL LOAD ITSELF ON THE TARGET COMPUTER AND COPY EVIDENCE OF ANOTHER CRIME. YOU WILL NOT BE ABLE TO VIEW THE EVIDENCE YOURSELF.**

**THE COMPUTER YOU SEEK WILL BE IN THE UPSTAIRS OFFICE OF THE ASHLANDS' HOME.**

**TO CLAIM THE REWARD, YOU MUST FOLLOW ALL INSTRUCTIONS EXPLICITLY. THIS IS YOUR ONLY WARNING!**

Eddie yanked the drive out of the PC. Jesus, the Gamemaster anticipated every damn move he made.

It worried him that he wouldn't know anything about the "crime" evidence he would be giving to Mike's dad. Could he trust the Gamemaster's promise that it wouldn't get him or Mike in trouble? He already screwed up his first attempt to frame Geoff.

He leaned back in the chair and closed his eyes. The thought of getting even more cash and finding out who was behind this whole Hoodlum scenario seemed much more important than the small risk that he might somehow cause pain or inconvenience to the Ashland family. And if this new evidence directly implicated Geoff in another crime, even better!

He shut down the PC and decided to pay the Ashlands a visit tomorrow. After all, he needed the trail camera to set his trap.

---

Though not as sunny as the previous Saturday, Eddie noticed Cindy walking out to the pool in her bikini for another day of sunbathing. Nice! He had already planned to mow the lawn today. As he pulled the mower and gas can out of the shed, the bucket with the Hoodlum laptop caught his eye. He remembered that he hadn't worked out a long-term hiding place for the money. Oh well. He supposed that could wait for now.

It took him about an hour to mow the lawn. Mowing the back yard seemed much more engaging than usual, since he could enjoy watching Cindy catch the rays. He didn't dare look for too long, though. She wore dark sunglasses, and he couldn't tell if her eyes were open or not. At one point she sat up to rub suntan lotion on herself. He imagined how incredible it would feel to apply it all over her beautiful body. Distracted by the thought, he pushed the mower over the only exposed root in the whole yard. The high-pitched shriek of the mower blade startled him back to reality. Cindy heard it too. She sat bolt upright and looked right at him. He grinned sheepishly and waved, and she waved back. He could feel his whole face flush. My God, what a hottie!

Eddie completed the row, still blushing, then swung the mower around for the next one. His heart nearly jumped out of his chest. Old Lady Lauffer was standing at the edge of her yard, shielding the sunlight with her hand and staring directly at him! At first, he thought she looked angry. Did she somehow know about him taking the mermaid? He forced himself to calm down. If she knew, the sheriff would have already paid him a visit. Right?

Back when Mr. Lauffer was alive, he used to always throw Eddie a big smile and friendly wave when they saw one another outside. But the Old Lady would drag him back indoors, as though he shouldn't associate with the simple peasants next door. Sometimes she offered a reserved wave herself, but never a smile or greeting.

Yet today her smile beamed like a gameshow host as he approached. He assumed she was going to ask him about the missing mermaid. Eddie figured he better get this over with. When he got to the edge of her yard, he released the handle to shut down the mower. He waved and started towards her. As soon as he did, she turned and briskly returned to her house. She never once glanced back. What the hell? She sure looked like she wanted to talk to him. Did she lose her nerve? He shook his head and plodded back to the mower. Sadly, he noticed Cindy gathering her things to go inside, too.

When he finished the yard, he rolled the mower back into the shed. To Eddie's surprise, the bucket with the laptop now had the lid removed and something was sticking out of it. It looked like a camouflaged case about three feet long, with a note on it. The camera! Mike must have dropped it off while he was mowing out front.

Mike's note begged him to be careful with the camera. He also cautioned Eddie that the camera made an audible "click" when it took each picture. If he set it up too close to the tee, someone might hear it and grab the camera. Made sense. Eddie read the instructions and tried taking a few shots of himself around the other side of the house. Mike was right about the clicking noise, but he estimated that his chosen spot for the camera would be far enough away.

According to the instructions, the pictures were stored on a removeable memory card inside the camera. You inserted the card into a small USB adapter, then plugged the adapter into a USB slot on any computer to view the images. He checked out his test pictures on the desktop PC, then deleted them. If the camera did fall into the wrong hands, he sure as hell didn't want to get busted at his own game! He packed it up, hopped on his bike and headed down the trail to the golf course.

Down at the hole four tee, he had to wait for two groups of golfers to pass through. He looked around to make sure no one was watching, then went to work. The ground was soft where he staked the camera, so he was able to sink it in nice and low. To keep it hidden, he had to set it back about a foot inside the small thicket. He worried that if it was windy, branches or brush might block the lens after the camera triggered. Ultimately the camera position would be a tradeoff between getting a good quality image and having it safely hidden from golfers and the Gamemaster. He lined it up as best he could and turned it on. This just had to work!

---

Getting into the Ashlands' house would be easy, but Eddie would have to do it while Mike's dad was home with his computer. Saturday afternoon should be a good time, he guessed. He looked through his own sliding glass door to the Ashlands' back yard. Cindy now floated on an air mattress in the pool, and her parents both sat reading at the table on the backyard deck. Couldn't ask for better than that!

He planned to get some homework done later, then work at the store until closing. Now was the time to move. If things went as planned, this task should be the easiest one yet.

With the thumb drive in his pocket, he stepped outside and walked over to the Ashlands' deck. "Hey, Mr. and Mrs. Ashland! How's it going?"

Murphy, their aging golden retriever, looked up at Eddie then dropped his head back on the deck.

"Hello, Eddie," Mrs. Ashland answered. "We're doing just fine. How 'bout you and your mom?"

Andrew gave Eddie a quick nod, but went back to reading the paper. Eddie assumed that he was still aggravated by the vandalism.

"We're doing well too," Eddie said. "Is Mike inside?"

"Go right on in, dear. I think he's in the basement working out."

Eddie stepped inside and removed his shoes per the Ashland family custom. Mary Ashland's house looked like a picture from a magazine, both inside and out. And no one wore shoes inside to mess it up. No one. Ever.

He could hear Mike's weights clanking in the basement. They had a well-equipped home gym down there, including a weight bench, squat rack, punching bag, exercise bike and a treadmill. His plan was to chat with Mike for a few minutes, then to ask to use the bathroom. He would then go upstairs and duck into Andrew's office. Should be a breeze!

He hadn't even made it to the bottom of the basement stairs when Mike called out.

"Hey Ghetti. Almost done. Can you give me about ten more minutes?"

"No problem. I'll wait in your room." Eddie climbed back up to the first floor and crossed to the second-floor staircase. This was ideal! Now he had all the time in the world. As he passed through the kitchen, he took a quick look through the glass doors to make sure everyone was still outside. He flew up the stairs three at a time.

Eddie knew the upstairs layout almost as well as his own house. While they were growing up, he had slept over too many times to remember and had explored every room. Andrew's office was the furthest door on the right. His laptop sat centered on the large desk, and Eddie wasted no time inserting the thumb drive.

All at once the realization of the risk he was taking washed over him. The moment seemed surreal, as if the snapshot memory of this moment could be a painful reflection for years to come.

This wasn't just about him getting in trouble. It could expose Mike too, and may even cost his father his job as club President. But that was only if the Gamemaster was lying, and he just couldn't believe that. Or did he just not *want* to believe it? Had his own selfish desire for money and for exposing the Gamemaster pushed him to this low point? Before he could talk himself out of it, he forced himself to focus. Like pulling a band aid, he told himself. Just do it quick!

He fumbled trying to open the laptop to power it on. Finally, the latch yielded and the laptop opened. He pressed the power switch, not allowing himself another chance to wimp out. The screen now showed the spinning skull "Hoodlum" emblem. That was unexpected! Hopefully the emblem would soon stop spinning and give some indication that the data had been successfully transferred. He had another terrible thought. What if the damn Hoodlum symbol didn't disappear for good once this thing finished? If things did go south and Andrew asked his son about the strange computer icon, Mike would know exactly who was responsible. Tense seconds passed while the frowning skull still spun. How long would this take? He was about to pull the USB drive anyway when the spinning finally stopped. The skull's angry scowl changed to a sinister grin, then disappeared.

Suddenly, he heard footsteps coming up the stairs. Jesus – he never heard the back door open! He could still hear the weights clanking down in the basement. It wasn't Mike. Shit! He snapped up the USB and closed the laptop. Andrew must be coming up to use the office. He couldn't get to the bathroom or Mike's room. They were both on the other side of the stairs! He didn't dare hide in the master bedroom; Andrew might go in there, too. He had to make a move -- right now!

He shot straight across the hallway into Cindy's room. There were clothes strewn all over the floor and her closet door stood open. He stepped as quietly as he could into the closet and pulled the door closed behind him. He could still see light through the gap between the door halves, and could hear the footsteps coming towards him.

Oh my God; it was Cindy! He could see her walk into the room and close the door. She must be coming into her bedroom to change! He realized that if she caught him peeping at her, not only were any hopes he ever had of dating her gone; he would probably be arrested! As much as he wanted to watch her undress, he turned away from the gap in utter terror. He could not even imagine the shame he would feel if he were caught. The Ashlands, his mother, kids at school, everyone. What could he do? Cindy was bound to open the closet to get fresh clothes. He wanted to burrow into some of the hanging full-length garments to hide, but he was afraid of making even the slightest noise.

He then heard the bedroom door open again and heard her footsteps in the hallway. Was she going to the bathroom? He had to get out now! Stepping carefully out of the closet, he crept up to the hallway door. Sure enough, he could see the bathroom door close just as he peered around her door. Taking soft but long steps, he zipped past the bathroom and dove into Mike's room to wait.

While sitting on Mike's bed, he tried to calm himself down. He'd done it! He wasn't sure what, exactly, but he had earned another fifteen hundred dollars, and hopefully gotten Geoff busted! But nearly getting caught in such a terrible situation reminded him again of Mike's warnings about the game. Was it really worth it? He wiped the sweat off his forehead, but he could not stop his heart from thumping in his chest. He reminded himself over and over that this task was in the bag, but he just couldn't relax. Unresolved thoughts and worries flashed through his mind like someone madly clicking a TV remote through channels in his brain.

How would the Gamemaster know the task had been completed? This task was different from the others. The previous tasks could be visually confirmed from a distance, but how could the Hoodlum game know that he had successfully loaded data onto Andrew Ashland's computer? Wondering about that reminded him of his own plan to uncover the Gamemaster's identity. He hoped that might soon pay off.

## Chapter 7 - Pushing New Limits

Eddie's mom had gotten up early on Sunday. She usually slept in on the weekends, but she told Eddie she wanted to make him a nice breakfast and spend some time with him. She knew he'd had a long week between school and work, and that he had to work again this afternoon. While he enjoyed his bacon, eggs and toast, she sat across from him with a cup of coffee.

"I hope you aren't working so many hours this week, Eddie."

"I'm not, Mom. And Eric let me come home early on Friday night, remember?" He felt pretty guilty getting the royal treatment. He'd been busy this past week alright, but mostly with Hoodlum related jackassery. He also found it ironic that she was worried about *him* working too many hours, while she herself did this routinely. "And I'll be home in time for dinner."

"Yeah, but I still worry that you're working too hard. You should be having more fun at your age. Maybe we can go to a movie this week, or take a drive to the lake? We haven't done that in a while, and it'll be winter before you know it."

"That'd be cool. Can we rent kayaks again?"

"I'll bet we could swing that," she said. "Or we could bring the bikes, if you think you can keep up with me."

They both laughed, remembering the last time they went. They had biked along the state park trail for about ten miles. Tina had struggled to keep up, then really fell apart on the ride back home against the wind. She claimed for days afterwards that the long ride had "permanently broken her ass."

Eddie helped with the dishes but was anxious to see if the Hoodlum game had acknowledged his latest task completion. Even more, he hoped that he'd caught the Gamemaster on the hidden trail cam. He thanked his mom for the breakfast and slipped outside to the shed.

Though it had been overcast all morning, the shed felt like an oven. Eddie decided on the spot to permanently relocate the bucket and Hoodlum laptop to the garage. Over the past week he'd noticed that his mother hardly used the garage at all, and there were a number of battered old cupboards he could use to stash the PC and bag with the cash. The money from his bedroom closet should be moved down there, too. He still wasn't thrilled about his cash storage situation, but again decided it would have to do for now.

He opened up the laptop and cycled through the startup screens. His heart sank when he read the message. He couldn't believe it! The Gamemaster had acknowledged the successful completion of the fourth task, but had switched the pickup location to the hole *three* tee. Shit! Did he discover the camera? How could he have known? Either Eddie hadn't hidden it well enough, or maybe the click that Mike had warned about had tipped off his intended target. Hopefully the camera was at least still there. If not, he would need to use some of his reward money to buy a replacement. And Mike would be pissed.

Eddie wanted to collect the additional reward money, but he was extremely disappointed about the failure of the trail cam plan. He didn't have enough cameras to cover multiple holes, and it was likely now the payoff location would change for every damn task. He still couldn't believe his bad luck. If only he had thought of the trail cam idea sooner!

He put the Hoodlum paraphernalia and cash in the oldest looking cupboard. A few partially filled oil cans and long forgotten windshield scrapers needed relocation, but it was otherwise empty. Judging by the dust and cobwebs, no one had opened any of these cupboards in years.

In spite of his disappointment, he would need to get moving. If he started now, he had just enough time to pick up the cash reward and the trail cam before work.

---

He soon learned that the hole three tee was quite some ways past the hole four tee. He picked up the envelope just as a group arrived at the tee. One of the old guys in the group watched him stuff the envelope into his shorts and bike off down the trail to the hole four tee. The old guy continued to watch him, and pointed him out to the other golfers in his group. Eddie realized he would need to be much more careful while doing anything suspicious around the golf course now. Everyone would be watching for the vandals.

With that in mind, he watched the group on the hole four tee from a distance. They eventually meandered down the fairway, and he zipped around the far side of the cart path to recover the trail camera – he hoped. Fortunately, the camera still sat in the thicket where he planted it. He would still need to clear the memory card before giving it back to Mike, though. This was no time to get sloppy!

Back in his garage he counted out the cash. Another fat looking stack of one hundred-dollar bills to add to his growing collection. Woohoo! He halfheartedly checked the Hoodlum laptop to see if the pickup had been confirmed. Not yet. Whatever. Now that his trail cam plan had been thwarted, his enthusiasm for unraveling the mystery of the game had diminished. Now it didn't seem like he would ever find out who the Gamemaster was, and the scare in Cindy's bedroom made him consider quitting altogether. He supposed he would need to at least read the next task, as always, and then decide.

Also, he was very curious about the "new evidence" that he had planted on Mike's father's computer. Asking Mike about any updates on Geoff's failed frame-up might be the only way to find out about any new developments. He'd have to be careful, though. If some surprising new evidence did come to light, especially on his father's computer under mysterious circumstances, Mike would figure out what had happened.

He pulled the memory card from the camera and brought it inside to the desktop computer to clear whatever it may have recorded at the familiar hole four tee. He was surprised to see that over forty pictures had been captured. He was just about to delete them all, then stopped. It would only take a few minutes to check over each picture, and he might see something interesting.

As expected, the first thirty or so of the images were golfers teeing off on hole four. No surprises there, except for the shot of one of the golfers taking a piss practically right on the camera itself! The camera positioning worked out better than expected for picture quality. It was easy to pick out details of the faces. If the Gamemaster was someone they knew, he believed the trail camera would have worked. If only the bastard hadn't switched pickup locations!

He scanned down the column of thumbnail images. Except for the last four images, the ones with the most recent timestamps, the golfer pictures all looked about the same. Slight variations in the lighting due to time of day, but otherwise the same -- golfers standing around the tee area with the woods and fairway in the background.

The last four mini-images looked as though they were taken at an entirely different setting, however. He opened the first of the four strange images to view it fully sized. It looked like a distant shot of a girl sunbathing near a pool. How the hell did that get there? He had made damn sure he cleared out all of the old images before setting up the camera, yet somehow there was an image of a bikini girl mixed in with the dozens of golfers. He opened the next picture, and nearly jumped out of his seat. It was a much closer shot of the same girl, and the girl was unmistakably Cindy! The timestamp on the image file was yesterday, while he was at the Ashlands. He couldn't believe Mike would do something like this, but who else knew about the camera? And who else could have taken this shot? Was he trying to scare him into quitting the game?

He had no clue what the next pictures were, but the mini thumbnails looked distinctly darker than the sunbathing girl thumbnails. When enlarged, picture number three was the angry burning skull Hoodlum emblem.

The goddamn Gamemaster! Did he hear the camera click while delivering the reward envelope? Or maybe he even watched Eddie plant the camera in the first place! Now the Gamemaster appeared to be taunting him. Or could it still be Mike? He wasn't a computer whiz like Steve, but he could easily have loaded these images on the camera memory card. It just didn't seem like something Mike would do.

The fourth and final image in the group looked like an individual slide from a PowerPoint presentation. Once again, the

Gamemaster had used the "ransom note" font with its random assortment of character types and letter sizes to display a message:

**NICE TRY, HOODLUM, BUT DON'T EVEN ATTEMPT TO OUTWIT THE GAMEMASTER! AS A TRUE HOODLUM, YOUR CURIOSITY IS UNDERSTANDABLE. YOU HAVE COME A LONG WAY, BUT YOU ARE NOT QUITE FINISHED. DON'T GIVE UP NOW! IF YOU ARE PATIENT AND PERSEVERE, <u>ALL</u> <u>WILL</u> <u>BE</u> <u>REVEALED</u> WHEN TASK NUMBER SEVEN IS COMPLETE.**

Now Eddie knew for certain that Mike didn't sneak the new images onto the camera. He would never have encouraged Eddie to continue with more tasks. This had to be a genuine message from the Gamemaster, and it seemed as though he was aware that Eddie might be losing interest. He may have also picked up on the fact that Mike had already quit, and wanted to inspire Eddie to keep going. This thought reinforced Mike's concern about just how closely the Gamemaster must be watching them.

But for the first time since he had started playing Hoodlum, the promise that "all will be revealed" after task seven. That was exciting news, if true! The idea of doing three more tasks by himself scared him, though. He recalled the terrifying moments in Cindy's closet.

Eddie deleted all of the images from the camera and wrapped it back up to give to Mike. He thought briefly of setting it up again at the fishing hole. That had been the site for a few package pickups, as well as the Hoodlum laptop itself. Ultimately, he decided against it. The thought of the Gamemaster taunting him again if the camera was discovered was just too embarrassing. Besides, he knew Mike would be anxious to sneak it back into his father's hunting supplies.

He would follow up with Mike later. For now, he would have to hustle to get to work on time. The cash pickup had taken longer than expected. He repacked the trail cam in the garage cupboard and raced upstairs to change for work.

---

To Eddie's surprise, his mother turned up at the grocery store about halfway through his shift. Since he would be home for dinner tonight, she picked out steaks for the grill and a few other groceries. He thought it seemed unusual she suddenly wanted to spend so much time with him. She had always been an attentive and loving mom, but typically didn't make much of a fuss over things like big breakfasts or backyard cookouts. Why the sudden interest? She had been acting a little strange around him lately. A crazy thought occurred to him. Could *she* be the Gamemaster? She certainly knew how to use a computer, but he didn't think she had any real programming experience. And why in God's name would she goad him into doing all of these bizarre tasks that could get him into serious trouble? It made no sense at all. Yeah, that was a crazy thought.

He did notice that she greeted Eric, his manager, warmly and must have exchanged a funny comment with him. They both laughed about something Eric said and continued talking. Eddie just knew they would make such a great couple. They had similar senses of humor, quoted old movie lines, liked a lot of the same music, and loved to read. Best of all, they were both the kindest and most generous people Eddie knew.

Eric's wife had passed away from cancer the year before Eddie had started working at the store. They had no children of their own, but Eric had served as a father figure for dozens of neighborhood kids that had worked at Silver's Grocery over the years. His "Silver's Kids" would often drop by to visit Eric at the store in later years -- home from college, introducing a fiancé, or showing off a new baby. And of course, Eric loved it. He would drop whatever he was doing to hug and visit with whomever he considered beloved members of his grocery store family.

Eric's confident, outgoing nature might be one of the few qualities that Tina Ponzino did not share with him. She had a few close personal friends from work, but acted quite shy around people she didn't know. It would be tricky to get these two together, but Eddie felt positive it would be worth it. Seeing the package of steak and the ears of corn in her arms gave him an idea. He could invite Eric over for a barbeque in their back yard sometime, along with a few of the kids from the store. Maybe the Ashlands, too. That would naturally pair Eric and his mother together for an evening, and maybe that would be enough to get the ball rolling. And it wouldn't look obvious to either of them that he was setting this up as a date. He could bring up the idea tonight with his mother, just to get her reaction. How come he never thought of this before?

Just the thought of getting his mom together with Eric lifted his spirits. He hadn't noticed until this moment how consumed with Hoodlum he had become, nor how depressed he felt since Mike had stopped playing. Collecting the latest reward did not deliver the same thrill that it once had. More than anything else, he resented feeling like he was just a helpless puppet of the Gamemaster. As Mike had worried, the possibility of blackmail loomed in the background. For a little while he thought he had an edge with his trail camera scheme, but now he was back to being a mindless slave to the game.

When he considered the three tasks he'd need to complete to get all the answers, he felt overwhelmed. A part of him hoped the next one would be so outrageous that he would just quit on the spot.

His mother caught his eye as she walked out. She pulled the steaks out of the top of the bag to show him, gave him a cheerful thumbs up and walked out to the car.

Eddie checked his watch and scanned the store, trying to estimate how many more customers would pass through his line before his shift would end. He didn't even have to ask Millie Jenkins, the only other cashier, if she was anxious to leave. She always looked grumpy, except when she talked about her grandkids.

The afternoon had not been busy at all, allowing his thoughts to drift back to Hoodlum. What did the game have in store for him next? On top of that, the promise of steaks on the grill fueled his desire to get back home.

Eddie turned back to his register just in time to see Eric talking to Emma, the friendly girl from his English class. He had seen Emma shopping at Silvers a number of times, but she typically accompanied at least one of her parents. The familiar cover of the cashier's training manual stuck out from her handbag. Was she planning to work here?

Eric turned and pointed to Eddie, and ushered her over to talk to him.

"Eddie, here, is one of our star cashiers, among other things. Eddie, this is…"

"Emma Stillman," Eddie finished. "We're in English together. How're you doing, Emma?" Eddie offered his hand.

Emma beamed a warm smile and shook his hand. "I'm doing fine, Eddie, how 'bout you?"

"Great, thanks!" He locked eyes with her for a moment, forgetting Eric was still standing next to both of them.

Eric cleared his throat, apparently to move the conversation forward.

"Well, that's great that you know each other already!" Eric gave Eddie a quick wink. "Emma will be starting next week as a cashier in training. I was going to have her watch you 'til the end of your shift, if you don't mind. She's already studied the training material, but she may have some questions about a few things the book didn't cover."

"Sure, no problem. Welcome to Silvers!" Eddie answered. The thought of working with Emma excited him more than he would have expected. Her short-haired head bobbed around with nervous energy as she took in the cash register environment. To Eddie, she somehow looked confident and vulnerable at the same time. She probably greeted everyone she met with her cheerful enthusiasm, but when she smiled and looked specifically at him, he felt like the most important guy in the world.

Eric walked back to the office, leaving them alone to chat and learn.

"You crack me up in English," Emma said. "So many of the kids are clueless, they don't even realize Mr. Entebbe is making fun of them. Every time he sticks it to somebody, he kind of sneaks a little look around the classroom to see if any of us picked up on it. He knows you get it. You even jump in sometimes."

"Yeah, I noticed that," Eddie laughed. "He must know you're in on it, too. He's great at those double meaning jokes – it's so hard not to laugh out loud."

"Oh, I know. Remember during '*The Canterbury Tales*' when Katie Rubins thought that – oh! You have a customer!"

Eddie turned to deal with the customer, engaging in small talk as he scanned and bagged the groceries. He knew he looked smooth, entertaining the lady's preschool son while scanning and bagging her groceries. He didn't want to overdo it, though. As much as he wanted to impress Emma, he wanted her to think of him as a friend – helpful and supportive, rather than snotty and aloof. She seemed so easy to talk to, and the more he thought about her the prettier she looked. Especially when she smiled or laughed.

The rest of the shift he previously dreaded now flew by in just moments. He didn't get much more of a chance to joke around with Emma before he had to close out. She'd asked a few serious questions about the job between customers, and he had explained some of the nuances in detail. He could tell she learned quickly. He wondered if she had a boyfriend. He didn't think so, but couldn't be sure. Even if she did, he imagined the two of them at least becoming close friends. And why not? They had quite a bit in common.

To his chagrin, Eric had Emma switch over to Steve Kagasimi when he relieved him on register. Steve also had a class or two with Emma, so Eddie felt a little pang of jealousy leaving the two of them behind. He tried to see if she acted as friendly with Steve as she had with him. He didn't think so, and Steve seemed almost laughably nervous about the whole thing. Emma looked serious now, and scribbled more notes in her binder.

"See ya, Steve! Good luck, Emma -- looking forward to working with you!" Eddie called on his way out the door.

Emma looked up from her notebook and warmed his soul with another big smile.

---

As expected, Tina had gone all out for the steak dinner. While he grilled the steaks, she prepared shrimp cocktail, mushrooms, corn on the cob and a pair of huge Idaho potatoes.

"Nice job on the sunset, Eddie Bear!" Tina elbowed the handle on the sliding door closed and gestured towards a sky streaked with brush-like strokes of soft pink and wispy light blue. She handed Eddie a platter for the steaks along with a cold root beer.

"All for you, Mom." Eddie answered. They clinked their root beers together and took a quiet moment to enjoy the sunset.

"Thanks for the steaks and stuff, Mom. This is really cool."

"You deserve it, Babe. You work so hard at your job and school, and even around the house. What would I do without you?"

"You're right, Mom. You'd be screwed. We shoulda got lobster, too." Eddie quipped.

Tina made her fake surprised face and jabbed her finger under his chin. No matter how old he got, he would always be ticklish there. He giggled like a little kid.

"Everything else is ready, wise guy. Bring the steaks over and let's do some serious eatin'!"

Tina had set up their little card table and two deck chairs for an outside dinner. The place settings featured the shrimp appetizer, and she had done her best to make it look like something you'd get in an expensive restaurant. She even used their fancy-looking plastic goblets, so they could drink their root beers like fine wine. It looked perfect to Eddie, even when he raised his eyes to the Ashlands' deck with their coordinated deck furniture, multi-burner grill and matching umbrella. As much as he envied his neighbors, he wouldn't trade times like this with his mom for anything.

Eddie knew most of the kids at his school would balk at the thought of spending a whole evening with their parents. Even though his mom worried about him a little too much and embarrassed him when she asked about girls in his class, he really did enjoy spending time with her. She always had funny comments during their movies, and he could joke around with her as though she was just one of his friends. He didn't think anyone else's parents were that much fun.

The food tasted fantastic, and the sunset lingered just long enough for them to enjoy every last bite.

"I'll clean up, Mom. You want to get the movie set up?"

"You bet – I can't pass that deal up. Harry Potter number four, right?"

"That's the one!" They had read and watched all of the Harry Potters, and had recently started re-watching the movies from the beginning.

As he washed the dishes, he considered telling her about Emma. He knew his mother would love to hear everything about her. She lived for this stuff! He worried that she would push him faster than he wanted to go, though. He decided to wait until things had moved a little further along before telling her.

He had hoped to catch Mike before dinner, to hear if there was any more news about Geoff. No luck though; the Ashlands' SUV was gone by the time he'd gotten back from the store. They often went out to eat on Sundays, or to visit Mike's grandparents.

As much as he enjoyed the steak dinner, it delayed him from finding out the next Hoodlum task. Now he would need to wait until after the movie to find out about task five, and probably until tomorrow at school to talk to Mike.

Worrying about Hoodlum didn't preoccupy his thoughts as much as it had before. His thoughts turned to Emma. He wondered what she would think of his involvement with Hoodlum. Would she be impressed that he had become sort of a neighborhood "bad boy" by doing these wild tasks, or would she think him foolish for jeopardizing his future so recklessly to earn a few extra bucks? He guessed the "foolish" option. She didn't seem like the type who would be impressed by vandalism or stealing. He looked forward to seeing her again, both in class and at work.

He opened the snack cupboard and spotted exactly what he had hoped for.

"Mom? You up for some popcorn, or too full?"

"You know me, Babe. I can *always* eat popcorn!"

Eddie closed the dishwasher, opened the plastic sleeve on the popcorn and slid the folded packet into the microwave.

As he walked into the family room, the arc of the Ashlands' returning SUV headlights swept across the wall behind him. Yes! He may get an update tonight from Mike after all…

---

After the movie, Tina yawned, delivered the empty bowls and cups to the kitchen and climbed the stairs to her bedroom.

"Love ya, Eddie Bear. See you tomorrow!"

"Love you too, Mom. Thanks for the great dinner!" Eddie answered. He remembered that the big garage door was still open, so hopefully he could catch up with Mike and get the details on the next task right from his new Hoodlum headquarters. He opened the door from the kitchen hallway and stepped into the dark garage.

He texted Mike to see if he could stop over. While waiting, he powered up the Hoodlum laptop. The pickup had to be acknowledged by now. He could not imagine what the next task could be, but mentally prepared himself to bail if it looked even slightly risky.

Before he even had a chance to check, he could hear Mike's footsteps on the driveway. He noticed it had gotten quite late. Mike would not have much time at all.

Mike stepped into the garage but seemed wary of entering too far.

"Hey Ghetti," he said. "How's it going?"

"Hey Mike. Not bad," he answered. He pulled the trail camera out of the cupboard and handed it to Mike. "No luck with this, though. The Gamemaster switched pickup spots on me."

Mike held his hands up, clearly showing he didn't want to hear any more about the game.

"OK, OK I get it. Can I just ask one question?"

Mike shrugged but didn't answer.

"Did your dad find out anything more about Geoff and the golf course?" Eddie asked.

"Nothing he told me about. He hasn't talked to me about it at all, and I haven't asked. I know they're already fixing it back up, but he's still totally chapped."

"OK, thanks. I still can't believe that crap."

Mike nodded, gave him a little salute with the trail cam and backed out of the garage into the night.

Eddie turned back to the Hoodlum laptop. He considered the possibility that Mike's father already found whatever he put on the computer. If it did further incriminate Geoff, he probably would have told Mike – but maybe not. If the mystery data somehow exposed him and Mike as the true vandals, however, his dad would *certainly* have confronted them. He supposed no news was good news, from that perspective.

He jumped through the startup screen, saw that the Gamemaster confirmed the reward pickup and opened the challenge for task five.

The Gamemaster promised $2000 for successful completion of the next task. He read and re-read the challenge in disbelief:

**GREETINGS, HOODLUM!**

**FOR TASK #5, YOU WILL ONCE AGAIN BE ASKED TO TRANSFER DATA FROM A USB THUMB DRIVE ONTO A SPECIFIC COMPUTER. AS BEFORE, YOU MUST NOT, UNDER ANY CIRCUMSTANCES PUT THIS THUMB DRIVE ON ANY OTHER PC! BY NOW YOU SHOULD TRUST THAT THE GAMEMASTER WILL NOT BETRAY YOU; BE ASSURED THAT THIS DATA WILL IN NO WAY IMPLICATE YOU OR YOUR PARTNER IN ANY WRONGDOING. BUT YOU MUST EXERCISE**

**<u>EXTREME</u> <u>CAUTION</u> IN EXECUTING THIS TASK. THE TARGET COMPUTER IS IN THE HOME OF RODNEY BLACKMOORE, AT 5036 FRONTIER LANE.**

**TO ASSIST YOU IN THIS MOST DIFFICULT CHALLENGE, THE GAMEMASTER HAS ARRANGED FOR THE FAMILY TO BE AWAY FROM THE RESIDENCE FOR THE EVENING. THIS WILL REQUIRE YOU TO COMPLETE THE CHALLENGE WITHIN A VERY SPECIFIC TIMEFRAME, HOWEVER. THE TASK WILL NEED TO BE COMPLETED BETWEEN 8 AND 9 PM ON THURSDAY NIGHT OF THIS WEEK.**

**AN ENVELOPE WITH THE USB DRIVE, A MEANS TO ENTER THE RESIDENCE AND SPECIFIC INFORMATION ABOUT LOCATING THE COMPUTER WITHIN THE HOME HAS BEEN PLACED IN THE LOCATION WHERE YOU FIRST DISCOVERED THE HOODLUM LAPTOP. BE SURE TO PICK IT UP BEFORE THURSDAY.**

**AS ALWAYS, GOOD LUCK, HOODLUM!**

Eddie powered off the laptop, slapped it closed and stuffed it back in the bag. Mike was right, this shit was just getting crazier every time. Rodney "Hot Rod" Blackmoore was the father of Tom Blackmoore, Geoff's friend and his ironclad alibi for attending a concert while the golf course crime took place. It made sense that planting some kind of evidence on his computer might somehow change the alibi, and again put Geoff back in the crosshairs. But the most important fact about Hot Rod Blackmoore, as far as Eddie was concerned, was that he was a *cop*. Sneaking into a close friend's house was bad enough. He could not even imagine himself breaking into a stranger's house, empty or not. And certainly not the home of a cop! Even the promise of $2000 could not justify such an enormous risk.

So, this is how it ends, he thought. He closed the garage door and tossed the Hoodlum bucket back in the old cupboard. He realized that the Gamemaster wouldn't even know that he had bailed until 9pm on Thursday, but so what? He'd made some decent money and experienced some epic adventures he could someday share with others. He still wished he knew who was behind all of this, and why. If he walked away, he may never find out. But whatever. He would just have to live with it. He killed the lights and walked inside to go to bed.

---

By Tuesday morning, Eddie had mostly forgotten about Hoodlum and the insane fifth task. He had worked the Monday night shift with Emma. Frankly, he could think of little else. Though he couldn't be certain from their brief time together, he got the sense that she wanted to be good friends, too. Perhaps more?

He tried to picture himself as her boyfriend – going on dates, meeting her parents, holding hands and, with any luck, exploring an intimate relationship. He found it both easy and pleasing to imagine. In the past, when he tried to envision a similar relationship with Cindy, it never seemed realistic. He no longer thought the awkward mismatch was due to her being "out of his league," though. They were just different in so many ways, and he realized he really didn't know Cindy as a person at all. He struggled to even imagine a conversation with her.

With Emma, on the other hand, he felt much more relaxed and natural. Though still nervous about talking to a girl at all, he could converse and joke with her almost as easily as he could with Mike or Steve. Unfortunately, his break times didn't overlap with Emma's last night, but he did get a chance to help her get started on her own register. She picked it up quickly and her perky personality resonated with every customer that she checked out. The entire mood of the store seemed to reflect her attitude. The usual sounds of crinkling bags, slamming register drawers and banging groceries faded beneath cheerful greetings, polite "thank-yous" and lighthearted laughter as customers passed through her line.

Between customers she and Eddie did enjoy a few moments of joking around. His heart soared every time she laughed at anything he had said.

He drifted through his morning classes in a daze, replaying their brief exchanges from last night in his head. Knowing he would be crushed if she said no, he wanted desperately to ask her out. He didn't think that would happen, but he had to consider the possibility. It occurred to him that he could ask Mike, the expert in such matters, for advice. Mike wouldn't understand his reluctance at all. He represented the opposite side of the confidence scale, and probably had never been nervous about such things. Still, he may have some good advice. He made a point to catch up with Mike after lunch. Last night he'd checked the work schedule, to see what nights Emma would be working. On Thursday night, he saw they would both work the late shift. Maybe that was his chance!

He rehearsed his greeting options to her in his head on the way to English. Though he didn't want to embarrass her by overdoing it, he wanted her to know he liked her. He wondered if she would even acknowledge their "workplace" acquaintance while in the school setting. Should he play it cool, in case she didn't want others to think she hung out with nerds? A sudden light jab in his ribs from behind jarred him from his thoughts.

"Hey Eddie!" Emma said, sunny smile a mile wide. "How's it going?"

"Oh – hi Emma! It's going great! How are you?" Eddie answered, relieved that the burden of starting the conversation had vanished. He tried to smile just as broadly, but it felt out of character for him. He wished he had worn something much cooler than his Star Wars shirt. She fell in step right beside him, and it occurred to him that he had never even walked together with a girl before. Even as just friends. The realization made him feel as though he had instantly taken a monstrous leap up the school's social ladder.

"Livin' the dream," she answered. "You working tonight?" Emma seemed so comfortable with herself, just strolling along and conversing as though they were the only people in the hallway. He hoped he could tap into that same sense of self-assuredness someday, but he knew he had a long way to go.

"No, just tomorrow and Thursday. You on tonight?"

"Yep! But I'm on Thursday night too. That's cool!"

"Yeah!" Eddie answered, with just the perfect level of enthusiasm, he hoped. He stopped to let her through the door to the classroom.

"OK, now. Remember Eddie; this is a very serious class. I don't want to see you laughing, smiling or having a good time. Is that clear?"

Before he could even answer, she jabbed him again and giggled her way to her desk. Their teacher, Mr. Entebbe, must have overheard Emma's comment. He looked as though he had his own funny comment to add, but another student interrupted him with a question. After that, he jumped right into the lecture.

For an old guy, Eddie thought Entebbe was pretty cool. He grew up out west somewhere, survived two tours in Vietnam as a marine, then moved to a small town in England. That's where he met his wife, who he claimed made him fall in love with her *and* with literature. He had written a few novels himself, then found his true calling as a teacher of English literature. Eddie and most of the sharper kids appreciated his unique style of teaching.

---

His dramatic and even bawdy narration of their reading assignments brought them to life, and anyone who was paying attention soon realized just how vulgar and entertaining "stuffy old British literature" could be.

While the students settled into their seats, shuffling textbooks and folders from bag to desk, Eddie openly gazed at Emma. She sat two desks in front of him and one desk to his left, so he could watch her without being obvious. And for pretty much the rest of the class, that's what he did. He recalled that less than a week ago, he had thought of Emma as "plain" looking, at least in a classroom with a high percentage of cheerleaders and other glamour-conscious girls. Now, with a more knowing eye, he could almost see a physical glow of selflessness and positivity in her that no girl in this classroom could ever hope to match. How could he have missed how beautiful she truly was? He wondered if others could see it too, or were they all as blind as he had been?

Entebbe must have said something amusing. Emma looked over her shoulder to catch Eddie's eye, laughing. He smiled back, though he had no idea what the joke was about. In fact, he had no idea what the topic of the lecture had even become. Thank God he didn't get called on; he would have looked like one of the morons that Emma and he ridiculed!

The thought he invested in the last few moments of class, thinking of a clever parting comment to Emma, was wasted. The shuffling stampede of feet, bookbags and bodies swept her away from him and down the hallway before he even had a chance.

---

Eddie didn't connect with Mike until after dinner. Mike had just finished a run and was walking his usual cool-down laps around the cul-de-sac. Eddie spotted him through the family room window, where he had just sat down to start some homework on the computer. He stepped outside and started down the driveway to intercept Mike before he got back to his house.

"Hey Mike! How's it going?"

"Hey Ghetti. I'm good."

Mike didn't look happy to see him at all. In fact, he looked like he wanted to just avoid Eddie entirely and get back inside.

"Got a minute?" Eddie asked, walking directly in his path.

"Sure. What's up?" Mike's eyes squinched up, as though preparing to cut the discussion very short.

"Don't worry. Nothing about the game. I promise."

Mike slowed, and appeared to soften somewhat.

"Stock tips? Weather forecast?" he asked with raised eyebrows.

"Close," Eddie laughed. "Girl advice."

Mike beamed at that.

"My man Ghetti, makin' the moves! Who's the lucky young lass?"

"You might not know her. Emma Stillson? She's a junior in my English class."

Mike closed his eyes and focused. Eddie imagined him flipping through a virtual rolodex of girls' names and faces. After a moment, he snapped out of his trance.

"Does she have kinda short hair, really smart? Says 'hi' to every person she passes in the hall?"

"That's her. She just started working at Silver's. She's really nice. And funny, too. I like her a lot."

"That's rad, Dude! You guys would be perfect together!"

"I think so too, but I'm worried about asking her out. I don't even know if she has a boyfriend."

Mike returned to his virtual girl catalog system.

"I'm not sure, but I don't think so. I don't see her with other guys in the hall, at least anyone in particular. And I don't remember hearing anybody I know talking about her. I'm thinkin' she's yours for the asking, Romeo!"

Hearing that from Mike raised his hopes into the stratosphere, but he still had concerns.

"How can I be sure, though? I'd hate to ask her out and then find out she really is seeing someone else. I don't think I could handle the embarrassment."

"Jesus, Ghetti. You'll have to risk it. You're a friggin' Hoodlum, remember?" He slugged Eddie's shoulder. "If she turns you down, don't act like it's the end of the world. Girls are flattered just to be asked. If she's already seeing someone, just be polite. Say something like 'he sure is a lucky guy.' She'll remember that. She might have someone else in mind for you, or if things go south with her boyfriend, you'll still have a solid shot."

"Yeah," Eddie said. "That's really good advice. I'm still nervous, though."

"I totally get it. You picture her telling her friends and laughing about it, right? I don't think this girl is like that, Ghetti. I don't know her much at all, but I'm betting she'd be totally into you."

"I sure hope so. Thanks, Mike."

"No problem. I'm really pumped for this to work out. Good luck!" Mike continued up his driveway, then suddenly stopped and turned back. He took a glance at his own house to make sure no one could hear him.

"Be careful, Ghetti. I haven't heard any more about the golf course damage, but my dad says they're watching the course and the whole neighborhood a lot more carefully now. They got some security cameras and a night watchman."

"I will, Mike. I promise." Eddie returned a thumbs up.

"Just be careful, Ghetti. I mean it. Ask this nice girl out and forget about that fucked up game."

Mike peeled off his sweaty running shirt and jogged straight through his garage to the pool.

Until that moment, Eddie really hadn't laid out his options like that. It seemed so obvious now! If he suddenly had an actual girlfriend, he wouldn't have much time nor interest in Hoodlum anymore. Instead of creeping through the neighborhood at night, praying no one would catch him, he could be watching movies, holding hands, and spending every free minute with Emma. And he would have someone to spend his newfound cash with, too! He made up his mind to ask Emma out on Thursday at work.

Feeling much more confident after his talk with Mike, Eddie walked back through his own garage and back to the desk in the family room. He had three Physics problems to solve. Now he just wanted to get them knocked out fast so he could start planning his big moment with Emma.

He powered up their old desktop PC, knowing it would take a few minutes to boot up. While he pulled books and his calculator out of his backpack, he could hear the disk drive revving up to speed. He clicked his name to access his desktop. Instead of his personalized desktop background of Jupiter and its moons, the screen hung up with a spinning cursor in the center of the screen. Great. Looks like the damn PC may have finally bit the dust. As he reached for the power switch to force a reboot, the spinning cursor transformed into the Hoodlum burning skull icon, and filled the screen. Jesus! This was his personal computer he shared with his mother. What if she had seen this? He wondered if he had caused this himself by trying to peek at the thumb drive before plugging it into Mike's father's computer, or if the Gamemaster could somehow access his personal computer on his own. That was a chilling thought.

The skull icon disappeared, but switched to the Hoodlum background screen with evil symbols around the border.

**GREETINGS, HOODLUM!**

**THIS IS A FRIENDLY REMINDER TO PICK UP THE PACKAGE AT THE DESIGNATED SPOT BEFORE THURSDAY. AS YOU KNOW, THE CHALLENGE MUST BE COMPLETED BETWEEN 8-9 PM ON THURSDAY NIGHT. THE PACKAGE WILL BE REQUIRED TO COMPLETE THE TASK, AND IT HAS NOT YET BEEN PICKED UP.**

**THE GAMEMASTER IS CONCERNED THAT YOU MAY BE LOSING YOUR NERVE. DON'T GIVE UP, HOODLUM! REMEMBER THAT ALL WILL BE REVEALED AFTER TASK 7 IS COMPLETE. YOU HAVE ALREADY MADE IT THIS FAR. IF YOU NEED ADDITIONAL INSPIRATION, CLICK THE BUTTON BELOW TO REMIND YOU OF WHAT YOU ARE CAPABLE OF.**

**KEEP THE FAITH, HOODLUM. PICK UP THE PACKAGE TOMORROW, AND BELIEVE IN YOURSELF!**

**KIND REGARDS,**

## THE HOODLUM GAMEMASTER

A glaring button labeled "INSPIRATION" flashed below the text.

Eddie hesitated before pressing it. He desperately hoped Mike was wrong, and the button would simply show a table listing each of the tasks completed, along with the cash reward earned. He knew he'd have to press it, dreading the worst.

As he feared, the button opened a full-sized video screen. He didn't recognize the location right away because of the strange angle. Eventually he realized the camera must have been placed at or near the top of the Sutter Valley entrance facade. He couldn't make out faces at first, but he knew exactly who the two boys on bikes were. They cruised around the intersection looking for witnesses and cars. Eventually they came into face view, before picking up the bag with spray paint, and finally climbing up to deface the sign. Shit! He fast-forwarded through enough of the Mermaid caper to see once again, both of their faces were captured on film. Further on, and most damning of all, a camera outside the greenskeeper shed showed the pair breaking in, then later exiting on the tractor, grinning like idiots.

He shut the video down, dimly aware his hand was shaking uncontrollably. He was fucked! He tried his mother's desktop, just to make sure she wouldn't see the Hoodlum logo or message. He was at least relieved to see both of their desktops had returned to normal. Not that he would be able to focus at all on his Physics homework tonight.

Eddie leaned back in his chair and grabbed his head. Did he have any choice at all now?

## Chapter 8 - The Fifth Task: Breaking and Entering

The crisp chill of autumn had found its way to Sutter Valley. Eddie nodded and pretended to appreciate the colorful changing foliage his mom pointed out during breakfast before she left. From his perspective, the day looked like total crap.

On top of the Hoodlum nightmare, which seemed likely to result in a life-destroying arrest, a number of other problems promised to make this day an epic disaster. For starters, he had done a really half-assed job on his Physics assignment. He knew if he could just push the Hoodlum stress from his mind for an hour, he could have figured out all of the problems. He just couldn't shake his panic. And Physics was his first class, so no hope of chipping away at it in between or during other classes. Not a huge deal by itself, but he had always prided himself on doing well in his science classes. Perhaps a lingering trait from his grandfather.

Beyond that, it just occurred to him that to complete the Hoodlum challenge, he would need to ask someone else to pick up his shift on Thursday night. Bad enough it was short notice, but now he wouldn't be able to work with Emma. It would be just his luck if someone else, someone like Steve Kagasimi, jumped his claim and asked Emma out before he did!

With these cheery thoughts in mind, he dumped his books into his backpack and opened the fridge to grab his lunch. His mother's favorite fortune cookie saying caught his eye, adding to his sour mood.

"Your future is an unwritten page, for YOU are in charge of your own destiny," seemed like a curse to him now. Admittedly, he had chosen his own path with Hoodlum by talking Mike into the first few challenges. At this point, however, he was decidedly *not* in charge of his own destiny. The Gamemaster had assumed that important role. And though the Gamemaster had not overtly threatened to share the video if he didn't accept the challenge, the implication was clear. Whatever trust he had placed in the Hoodlum game before had now vanished. He would just need to accept whatever horrors the next challenges had in store. The Gamemaster had promised "all would be revealed" after task seven, but that could be a total lie. And even if it was, what could he do? He had laughed at Mike's prediction about "killing people by Christmas," but now the thought didn't seem so funny at all.

He stuffed his lunch into his pack and dragged himself out the door to begin what was sure to be a grim day.

---

As it turned out, his shortfall in Physics went undetected. A few of the other students had whined about the difficulty of the problems, so their teacher allowed them to work out the problems in class as teams. His team did well, as expected. Steve had completed all of the problems on his own, of course. As a bonus, Steve agreed to take Eddie's Thursday night shift, and even offered to give up Saturday night as a trade, if Eddie wanted. Though he agreed to the shift swap, Eddie did feel a tinge of worry about Steve and Emma. He knew Steve had always been timid around girls, even worse than him, but what if he had the same thoughts about Emma? Her friendly nature made her a likely target for guys that would otherwise shy away. The fact that Emma and Steve would now be working together on Thursday night worried him even more, but what could he do? Unless…he asked Emma out today. The thought scared him at first, but in the face of everything else going on, maybe this would be the perfect time! Mike's advice had helped him get past most of his rejection worries. And Mike thought she would say yes. That meant a lot. If he had asked Mike about a girl that really was out of his league, Mike would have coached him through a more conservative approach, or suggested another girl. Yeah. Today would be the day.

His next class, French, was his least favorite. Foreign language was one of the few subjects that did not come easily to him, and he felt like an ass trying to pronounce words he didn't understand. Reciting dialogs in class embarrassed him, and he thanked God that Emma wasn't in this class with him. He could picture her speaking it perfectly, and trying not to laugh when it was his turn. He used what time he could to plan his big proposal. He couldn't count on running into her before English, so he would have to catch up to her right afterwards, maybe at her locker. He really didn't want to ask her in front of other people, but asking her today meant giving up on the preferred isolation of the store break room. Oh well. Once again, just like pulling a band-aid. He just prayed he wouldn't get tongue-tied at the critical moment and look like a complete idiot.

Sure enough, Emma had already taken her seat by the time Eddie got to English. He tried to imitate one of her big smiles, but it still felt so weird to him. Nonetheless, she smiled back and winked as he took his seat and unpacked his books. He spent the bulk of the class daydreaming, trying to think of witty segues into his big proposition. Entebbe surprised him with a question about "Paradise Lost," and he had to stammer his way through an answer. He eventually worked it into a credible response, but Entebbe must have sensed that he hadn't been listening. He wondered if Emma had noticed, too. Dammit! He forced himself to pay strict attention for the rest of the class.

Just like Tuesday, Emma dashed to the front of the classroom and through the door when the class had ended. Eddie had to wait for two lethargic seniors in the desks in front of him to get out of the way before he could join the chase. He knew Emma must be going to lunch now, but she would probably stop by her locker first to unload her English books. Unfortunately, he had no idea where that was.

Then, a lucky break! He spotted her bobbing head moving down the hall towards the cafeteria. As Mike had observed, she exchanged cheerful greetings with an astonishing number of people, including two teachers and a custodian. Each person she greeted visibly brightened as she walked by. It was as though Emma was surfing on a wave of benevolence that washed over everyone she passed.

Eddie couldn't catch Emma without blasting his way through the crowd. He didn't want to seem desperate, but he did want to catch her soon. She might be in a hurry to meet up with her lunch friends, and he didn't want to take up too much of her time. She did pass the cafeteria, he noticed, so she must be going to her locker.

The flow of students dwindled as he followed her down the stairs to the lone hallway at the far end of the building. No wonder he seldom saw her outside of class! He didn't even know there were lockers this far off the beaten path. This was the hallway that led to the music and art classrooms where he ventured only for school-wide assemblies. In this hallway only a few students stood fumbling with locker combos and lunch bags. Nice! She finally stopped at the absolute last locker in the hall and spun the knob of her combo lock.

"Hi Emma!" he said, trying to sound friendly and confident at the same time.

"Hey Eddie! What are you doing down here, in the forgotten catacombs of Sutter Valley High?"

"I was actually following you."

"Wow!" She laughed as he approached. "I've got my own stalker?"

"Uh, yeah! I guess I'm not very good at it, though. A good stalker is not supposed to be noticed."

"Oh, well I hope I didn't blow it. I'd hate to lose my first stalker so soon."

"No, I'm the one that blew it. I should have worn a disguise."

"That might have worked. Except now it's too late. Your cover is blown."

"True story. I guess I'll have to confess. I really came to ask you out. I mean, to ask if you if you'd like to go to a movie or something with me."

"Oh, how sweet! That would be great – I'd love to!"

Emma's face lit up even brighter than Eddie thought possible. He felt an indescribable blend of happiness and relief. Again, he was surprised by how easily he could talk to her.

"Awesome! Are you free Saturday night?" He realized he'd been so worked up about asking her out that he hadn't even looked at the movie choices.

"I sure am! In fact, if you don't have any lunch plans, I'm sure you would be most welcome at our lunch table."

That drove it home for Eddie. He could imagine her agreeing to go out on a date with him out of pity or general kindness, but now she was including him among her lunch friends.

"I would be honored. And I've already got my lunch with me. I do have one request though."

"Of course. What's your request? Fine wine?"

"That would be fine indeed! Your table must get much better service than mine. But I was really just hoping you wouldn't introduce me to your friends as your stalker."

Emma giggled and slugged him lightly on the arm.

"You're too much. Well, let's get goin'!"

She closed her locker and they walked together back down the hallway.

Eddie had always thought the expression "walking ten feet off the ground" was a corny phrase to describe someone's happiness, but damned if that's not exactly what it felt like to be walking down the hallway next to Emma.

---

The rest of the school day did nothing to diminish Eddie's spirits. Even the thought of picking up the Hoodlum package didn't depress him as much as it had this morning. He couldn't get over the fact that the same girl he had been so worried about asking out actually invited *him* to *lunch*. He bounced his way down the trail to the fishing spot, replaying the whole lunch scene in his head.

Emma's usual lunch crew sat among a small group of tables away from the central cafeteria. Eddie had passed by this side room countless times without ever noticing the people eating there. Over the past few years, he had always assumed his own table of science nerds, computer geeks and video game junkies represented the Sutter Valley High misfits. But when he entered the side room section for the first time, he realized his own "table o' nerds" wasn't even in the running. To his embarrassment, he suddenly understood how racially segregated Sutter Valley actually was. Two of the tables appeared to be exclusively occupied by minority students; what few there were in the community. At another table, furthest back, sat Jerry Quinn in his wheelchair. He looked down at his food, sitting alone, not eating. Eddie had seen him in the halls between classes but had never talked to him. Like most other students, he always avoided eye contact and did his best to pretend Jerry didn't even exist.

Across from Jerry's table sat a table of three students that looked like textbook misfits. One girl was quite heavy, and the clothes she wore did nothing to hide it in any way. She wore glasses and a grouchy expression. Directly across from her sat another heavyset girl who was more nicely dressed. Eddie thought she might be in his French class, but he didn't remember her name. Was it Angela? At the far end of the same table sat a tall boy. Eddie did not recall ever seeing him in school before, but was pretty sure he shopped with his parents at Silver's. The tall boy stared straight ahead, unblinking as he fed himself like a robot. He mechanically moved his arm in only perfect vertical or horizontal planes, opening and closing his mouth on the food before returning the fork to the plate for another robotic bite.

Based on Emma's current heading, this table of misfits was their destination. Emma had introduced her friends, and was able to get them all to at least say hello to Eddie. Even the robotic boy broke from his ritual when Emma asked him how his day was going.

As Eddie sat down, Emma set her lunch down across from him and walked over to say something to Jerry Quinn. She motioned over to their table, but Jerry shook his head. She asked again but got the same response.

While Emma walked back to their table, Eddie mentioned to Angela that they were in French class together. Angela responded with a nod, and that was it. Emma sat down and told Eddie that Jerry would never sit with them, and it made her sad to see him sitting alone. She still invited him every day.

Eddie tried to say something, but realized he was too choked up. The girl he had recently considered somewhat plain had become the self-appointed mother of these lost souls. He believed that they could all see her warm glow; her genuine care for people in need that he could now see, too. Maybe this table of misfits was where he truly belonged. He wasn't sure about that, but he was sure that he wanted to be with Emma. He didn't think that he could ever match the comfortable, caring way she had with people, but he promised himself that he would try to be more like her.

"You're such a good person, Emma," he finally got out. He never considered himself to be overly sappy or dramatic, but he felt tears welling in his eyes.

"Oh, thank you Eddie," she said. She looked like she was tearing up herself. "You just made my day."

"You already made mine," he answered. Without even thinking, he reached across the table and squeezed her hand.

Even now, hours later, the memory of touching her hand, and of her hand squeezing back was strong enough to dispel whatever evil the Hoodlum game had in store for him. After watching Emma today, he knew for certain he could never tell her about his involvement with this game of crime and greed. He didn't even care anymore about finding out who the Gamemaster was, or why he was putting him through this ordeal. He just wanted it to be over, and to spend as much time with Emma as he possibly could.

The envelope sat in the usual clump of grass. Eddie looked around, more wary than ever that the Gamemaster would be watching, or at least taping him on camera. A mother muskrat swam near the far side of the pond leading a parade of four or five babies behind her. Man, he used to love fishing down here. Now it would never be the same.

Back in the garage he opened the envelope, pulled out the house key and thumb drive and read the instructions. The Gamemaster reminded him that everyone would be out of the house between 8 and 9pm tomorrow night. He would need to enter the four-digit code on the alarm keypad to enter the house. The computer was located in a home office on the first floor. Page two showed a detailed view of the first floor, with positions of the keypad and home office highlighted. Jesus, if the Gamemaster had access to all of this information, what the hell did he need Eddie for? Based on what he could remotely do to Eddie's home computer, the Gamemaster could have probably loaded this crap directly onto Hot Rod's PC without having to even get out of his chair. Instead, he went to all the trouble of setting up this weird game, finding out the alarm code, printing out maps and instructions, somehow acquiring a house key and then relying on a kid who may not even have the balls to complete the task.

The only possible reason that Eddie could think of was Mike's theory. He would take video of Eddie breaking and entering -- an even more serious crime than the golf course vandalism. Eventually, the Gamemaster would have enough evidence on Eddie to get him to do whatever he wanted. But even knowing that, what could he do? If he bailed now, the Gamemaster had enough on him to destroy not only his own future, but Mike's as well. He really had no alternative but to proceed with this high stakes break-in. And God only knew what the next two tasks would involve.

---

Thanks to another lunch with Emma on Thursday, Eddie had suppressed thoughts of the upcoming Hoodlum challenge until after school. He finished his homework while Tina pulled together a tossed salad and frozen pizza for dinner.

Now that his date with Emma was a lock, he decided he could let the cat out of the bag. He finished his second slice of pizza and looked straight at his mother, trying to decide how to tell her.

"What is it, Eddie?" she asked mid-bite. "Oh my God – you didn't enlist, did you?"

Eddie almost laughed, watching her ramp up to a full panic in mere seconds.

"No, Mom. It's a good thing. I'm going on a date Saturday night."

Just as quickly, Tina transitioned from horrified to overjoyed.

"Oh, Eddie, that's wonderful!"

Eddie felt a little offended, as though maybe his mother thought he could never get a girl to date him. Had she really worried about that? Now, she looked as though she wanted to climb over the table to get to him.

"Well, tell me everything! Who's the girl? How did you ask her? Do I know her parents? Come on, Kiddo, you're killin' me here!"

"OK, OK. She's a girl in my English class. Emma Stillson. She just started working at Silver's, too. She's really, really nice. I know you'd like her."

"I'm so happy for you, Eddie. Do you have a picture? I can't wait to meet her!"

"Take it easy, Mom. It's just our first date. I don't want to scare her off. We're just going to a movie. If that goes OK, maybe we could have her over for dinner sometime. I think I have a picture of her in my yearbook." He sprinted to his room to grab last year's book.

It took Eddie a few minutes, but he did find Emma's picture in a few different places in the yearbook. Only the seniors got the individual full-face shots, but he remembered her telling him at lunch that she played flute in the school band. Sure enough, there were three pictures of her on the band photo pages; all of course featuring her signature smile.

"Oh, she's adorable Eddie! She works at Silver's and she's smart, too? Oh my God, I love her already. We've definitely gotta have her for dinner."

"Yeah, she's pretty awesome. I think the dinner thing would be cool, Mom, but just don't overdo it, OK?"

Eddie knew his mother would be excited, but she was practically foaming at the mouth.

"I promise. I'll be very cool. This is just so exciting!"

Tina turned up the radio and bumped her butt into Eddie to the rhythm of the "Sultans of Swing" while they washed the dishes. Seeing her this happy almost made him forget about the next Hoodlum challenge, now only a few hours away.

---

Eddie sat on his bike in the garage, mentally reviewing his plan of attack. His mother assumed he was on his way to work; he never changed the original Silver's schedule he'd posted on the fridge last Sunday.

He decided to stake out the Blackmoore house from the woods behind their house twenty minutes or so before eight pm. The Gamemaster had promised an empty house by then, but Eddie wanted to see the whole family leave for himself. He had looked up a satellite view of the neighborhood and noticed the Blackmore's back yard closely bordered the edge of the clubhouse parking lot. If he approached from the parking lot, he would just need to cross through about forty yards of woods to look down on the back yard. He figured coming in from the back would be much less conspicuous than riding up their driveway on his bike. It would also give him a decent view of whatever might be going on in neighboring houses.

He had taken Mike's warning about the new video cameras and the night watchman to heart. In addition to his dark clothing and hooded sweatshirt, he added a winter face mask to his supplies for tonight's caper. He didn't think the club would waste money on surveillance for their empty parking lot at night, but didn't want to take any chances. On top of that, wearing the mask should at least prevent the Gamemaster from getting even more video of him performing additional crimes. He hadn't worn the damn thing since sledding as a little kid, though, and it squeezed his head like a grape when he pulled it over his face. For the ride up, he decided to leave the mask off.

Eddie checked his pockets for the USB stick, the key and the paper with the alarm code and floorplan. He really didn't need the paper; he had committed the code and house layout to memory. Playing it over in his head one last time, he coasted down the driveway.

The bike trip to the clubhouse seemed endless, even using the Grassy Loop shortcut. As he passed by the St. Vincents' house, he noticed movement inside. Hopefully that's where they would stay. Next door, a towering four-door pickup stood waiting in the Blackmoore driveway. Eddie couldn't see any movement in the house, but could hear voices. Clearly, they had not yet left. As far as Eddie could tell, no neighbors lingering outside or walking along the street. At least for now.

He had to stand up on the pedals to climb the steep lane to the clubhouse. One lone car remained in the parking lot, and a few lights shone from within the clubhouse itself. The wooded edge of the parking lot that Eddie cared about had no lights whatsoever. Good deal. He dismounted and hid his bike just inside the tree line.

Until now, he hadn't felt too nervous. As soon as he broke through the woods and looked down at the line of backyards, though, his stomach clenched hard. He spotted the yard with a massive swing set and above ground pool. The Blackmoore place. He worked his way along the edge of the trees, keeping just inside their cover. Seeing the actual scene of the crime in the darkness filled him with an unshakable sense of dread. He checked his watch -- still fifteen minutes to go. Man, having Mike along would have made this so much less terrifying.

Lights inside the Blackmoore house were turning on and off in different rooms. From this angle he couldn't see the truck in the driveway, but he could hear vehicle doors opening and slamming closed. He waited several minutes. One light remained on inside the house, but all else had gone dark. A moment later, an engine started. The Blackmoores' pickup slowly accelerated down the road. Unfortunately, Eddie couldn't tell for certain if all four seats were occupied. He sure hoped so, though he could not imagine how the Gamemaster had arranged for the empty house at precisely this time. The thought both awed and frightened him.

He had already planned to sneak around the side of the house away from the St. Vincents'. He knew the families were close, and probably looked after each other's houses while they were away. A few of the homes had backyard floodlights, but they focused pretty tightly on their own decks. He left the safety of the woods, pulled the facemask over his head and crept down the hill to the house.

When he arrived at the front corner of the house, he stopped to peek into the only lighted room. It looked like an empty living room. No signs of anyone that he could see. Also, no activity at either neighbors' homes or at the house across the street. That gave him a little boost of confidence.

Up on the front porch, he knew he could be seen by anyone in the area – if anyone happened to be watching. He worked fast, typing the code into the alarm system. He noticed that the alarm itself was the same brand that Mike's house used – O.L. Security. Eddie had a little experience with that one. Whenever the Ashlands went on vacation, he would feed their dog and water the plants. He pressed "Enter" after the code and waited for the happy double chirp.

To his horror, the display switched from "ARMED" to "STANDBY." Would it activate, or alert the Blackmoores by cellphone? Jesus. This challenge could end real quick. After several tense seconds, the display returned to "ARMED." He carefully and deliberately pressed each digit once more. This time he was rewarded with a double beep and the message "DISARMED." Thank God.

He had to unlock both the doorknob and a deadbolt with the key. As soon as he slipped inside and closed the door, he could hear the unmistakable sound of paws walking towards him. He froze. This was an important detail that the Gamemaster had neglected to mention!

He pictured a hulking German Shepard police dog ripping his limbs off one at a time. While his body tensed for the attack, a small part of his mind wondered. What would they think happened when they found his mutilated body in their house? He supposed they would eventually identify him, unless the dog mauled him beyond recognition. What would they make of the mysterious USB, and the fact that he had a house key and floor plan? Or would the dog eat all that, too?

He could still hear the paws, now dancing around on the wood or linoleum floor, but not getting any closer. When he finally braved a look, he could see a gate blocking the stairs where the dog hopped back and forth, waiting to be released. The "killer police dog" turned out to be a large but friendly golden retriever. Better yet, he didn't seem to mind that Eddie was an unwelcome stranger in the house. That was very good news, since he needed to go down those same stairs to get to the office.

Eddie's hands shook as he prepared to straddle the dog gate. Too many scares already. He now wished that he had taken a piss in the woods before starting the whole affair. But using one of the Blackmoore bathrooms was out of the question. He wanted to finish the job and get the hell out of here as fast as he could.

Eddie threw a leg over the gate and took a moment to pet the excited dog. Even with the limited lighting, he knew exactly where he was going. The dog followed him for a moment, but then returned to his post at the top of the stairs. As promised, the computer sat atop a large desk in Hot Rod's home office. Though he couldn't make out many details, he could see the office walls lined with awards and pictures of fellow state troopers. The far wall of the office featured pictures of kids' sports teams and a shelf full of trophies. Eddie had forgotten that Rod was also a Little League coach. Another pang of guilt settled over him. He hoped this USB thing wouldn't get Hot Rod in trouble. He had always been kind to Eddie, and seemed like a genuine good guy.

He had to grope around a little while to find a USB port, but was rewarded with the Hoodlum burning skull logo as soon as he plugged it in. Just like at the Ashlands', the download seemed to take forever. He glanced out the high window, praying to not see headlights. Finally, the angry skull morphed into the sinister grinning skull, and the screen went blank. Eddie wasted no time grabbing the thumb drive and bounding up the stairs. He gave the dog a parting pat on the head and slung his leg back over the pet gate to the main floor. The dog whimpered when he realized Eddie had no intention of letting him out, but didn't bark.

Eddie scanned the neighborhood through the side window for any movement outside the house. Nothing. He closed the door behind him, taking care to re-lock both the doorknob and the deadbolt with the key. Checking once more behind him, he typed the code into the alarm system to return it to the "ARMED" state. The goddam facemask was not only tight, but now made his face itch like hell. He didn't dare take it off yet, though. He made his way around the house to the backyard, then started up the hill to the woods.

"Hey!" someone shouted behind him.

Shit! He'd forgotten to check the other backyards before starting up the hill. Someone was smoking on the back deck of the St. Vincent's. Probably Geoff's dad.

"Hey you! In the Ninja getup!" he shouted again. "What the hell're you doing? This is private property!"

Lights started turning on in other houses, and he heard at least one sliding door open. He sprinted for the tree line, hoping no one was planning to chase him. Now he really had to take a leak!

Once safely in the trees, he risked a look back. No one had pursued him up the hill, but he could see Geoff's dad standing in the Blackmoores' yard, yelling to a neighbor on another deck. After a moment, he pulled his cell phone out of his pocket and made a call. Hot Rod? The cops? To Eddie, it really didn't matter which. He had to get the hell out of there right now.

The two things he wanted to do the most were to take a piss and to rip the stupid mask off his head. Both would have to wait. He grabbed his bike and considered his options. If he took the road back, the way he came, he would have to ride directly in front of the same houses he had just fled. Even if Geoff's dad hadn't figured that out, he might still run into either the Blackmoores or the cops, whichever Geoff's dad had just called. And if they stopped him in his "Ninja getup," with a house key and floorplan to Hot Rod's house in his possession, he'd be screwed.

On the other hand, he could ride past the far end of the clubhouse and onto the course itself. But that meant risking detection by the security cameras and night watchman that Mike had told him about. He still had the facemask on, though, so he wasn't too worried about the video cameras. The night watchman could be a problem, but he decided to risk it.

He skirted around the far side of the parking lot, outside (he hoped) the range of the few lights that remained lit inside the clubhouse. Not being a golfer, he had no idea where the paved cart paths would actually take him. He knew the general direction of his street, however, and anyplace was better than where he was now. He rode as fast as he dared in the darkness. He almost lost it twice when the path turned sharply, but eventually arrived at the familiar section of fairways near his own house. As he crested the trail that led to his cul-de-sac he saw the flashing lights of a police car whip by the far end of his street, undoubtedly on the way to the Blackmoores' place.

He pedaled madly across the front yard and around to the back of his house. In a single continuous movement, he slid off the back of his bike, whipped the stinking mask off his head, and took the longest piss of his life right on the side of the rusty shed. Holy shit, what a night! He stood panting like a rabid dog, his heart pounding with no hint of settling down soon. Eddie turned to look at the Lauffer's vacant fountain, where the silhouette of the Mermaid had dominated the surroundings for so long.

At the time, the thought of that little challenge had scared him. Eddie remembered how excited and proud he felt after they'd pulled it off. Things seemed so different now. Of course, having a Hoodlum partner was a big part of that, but the stakes had also amped up considerably since then. Hoodlum had become much more than a game.

His mind flashed back to his lunch with Emma, and her natural devotion to kindness and caring.

Damn. He sure could use one of the Ashlands' beers right now.

## Chapter 9 - Collateral Damage

Andrew Ashland finished his shower and started his dressing ritual for the day. Today was no ordinary day; this afternoon he would present this year's Sutter Valley Golf Club business results to the board. Though he always dressed impeccably for club business meetings, today's presentation warranted his finest suit. Mary knew this and had already lain it out for him, along with his favorite tie and cuff links.

He certainly hadn't lost any sleep over today's big show. Andrew felt confident his presentation would blow the board members away. He had made a few controversial decisions this past year, and today's report would show that his decisions had paid off well. The club board loved him as President already, but it always felt good to remind them he was worthy of their adoration – and his ample paycheck.

He looked himself over in the mirror as he tweaked the knot on his tie. For a man his age he still looked sharp, but he noticed dark circles and puffiness under his eyes. The last few weeks had been tough.

First of all, the dipshit kids that had used one of the club's own tractors to trash the green had aggravated him more than he thought possible. The damage to the course hurt him personally, and the fact that they hadn't caught the bastards yet infuriated him. More than anything he wanted to drag whoever did this, or more specifically their parents, through the Sutter Valley gutter of shame. He and Mary had raised their own kids to be responsible citizens, and he expected every parent in the community to do the same. After all, without rules, what kind of madness would this world collapse into? He had approved the head greenskeeper's plan to beef up security, but in truth he had little hope they would ever catch the bastards.

The other crisis he had to deal with was his own damn fault. Several weeks ago, after years of casually flirting with his secretary, he had finally given in to temptation. How could he have been so stupid? Jennifer Blackmoore looked like a fashion model with an exquisite face to match, but what had intrigued him the most was her aura of subtle decadence. They had shared countless off-color jokes and double entendre comments during their business meetings, lunches and parties together. She would just smirk and look at him with those sultry dark eyes, wordlessly inviting him to give in to his lust.

So ultimately, give in he did. While pulling together the numbers for this same presentation, both he and Jennifer had stayed late. They had helped themselves to a few self-served drinks from the bar, invoking his "presidential status" as justification. He'd kissed her quite spontaneously, and she had led him to the women's lounge. Though well furnished, the lounge was no honeymoon suite. The small couch felt awkward, but Jennifer's intensity more than compensated. Andrew could not remember a time when he had felt so passionate and alive! But did she expect a serious relationship, or was she just looking for fun? He honestly couldn't tell. They both knew they couldn't linger afterwards, since they had already stayed so late. Mary had been upset about having to serve him a cold dinner, but seemed to understand. She knew how important this presentation was.

Despite the nagging guilt he felt the next morning, he could not wait to be with Jennifer again. They repeated the scenario several times over the next few weeks, becoming bolder and wilder with various locations in the clubhouse. But haunted by his conscience and love for his wife, the forbidden thrill of making love to this dark-eyed goddess began to ebb.

Andrew truly loved his wife and wouldn't hurt her or his family for the world. Mary most certainly did *not* exude any aura of decadence; the woman was the very face of selfless service to family, church and community. He loved her for that, and always would. And he was aware of the hypocrisy of his attitude about social propriety in light of his sinful tryst with Jennifer. He had to end it immediately. But he also had to do it delicately. He needed her as a secretary, and he wanted to keep the friendly professional relationship they had shared in the past.

To make matters worse, he and Mary frequently saw Jennifer and her husband socially. Though he didn't consider Roddy a close friend, they had played golf together a few times and often met as couples for barbecues, happy hours, fundraisers and school functions.

The few events that both couples attended since the affair had seemed excruciatingly stressful, but he felt confident neither Roddy nor Mary suspected a thing. He sure as hell didn't want Roddy coming after him. The guy was a big dude, and a cop to boot. Though he hadn't seen it himself, he'd heard that "Hot Rod" had quite a temper when provoked. He wondered if that little issue may have driven Jennifer to look outside of her marriage for love.

As fate would have it, Andrew had ended his affair with Jennifer the very same day that the vandalism to the course occurred. He worried that she might cause a scene, or threaten to expose their relationship. He had waited until everyone who worked in the clubhouse had left. To his surprise, she took his rejection without much drama at all. As always, he had rehearsed his monologue many times, and had prepared for the full range of her possible reactions. He did not expect the indifferent shrug. He wondered for the first time if he had been her only fling. Though mildly hurt by her casual attitude, he supposed that this was ideal. They could easily fall back into their innocent flirting and joking from this standpoint. He had gotten off easy!

When he learned of the vandalism to the course the following morning, he thought for certain it was Jennifer -- she hadn't taken the breakup as well as he'd thought.

His first instinct was to keep the whole thing quiet, fearing exposure, but the greens team had already produced proof that the St. Vincent kid had done it. That didn't surprise him at all. Geoff had always seemed like a mean, somewhat oafish kid. He had recently overheard Mike and Cindy talking about him; both agreeing that they didn't like him at all. And the dumbass kid had left a trail of self-incrimination a mile wide! His father's bolt cutters next to the shed and his student ID card left at the scene of the crime. Jesus, could the kid be any more stupid? Probably drunk or high.

Andrew had called Miles St. Vincent, Geoff's father, to confront them with the evidence. His initial fear about Jennifer returned when Roddy turned up alongside Geoff and Miles at the clubhouse entrance an hour later. What the hell was going on? Roddy had vouched for Geoff, to his astonishment, and had a pretty solid alibi for the kid for the whole night. But it didn't make any sense! They claimed someone was trying to frame him, and even presented the broken shed lock and tractor key that were supposedly "planted" near Geoff's front porch. His gut told him the frame-up scheme was a wild fabrication, but he really couldn't contradict Roddy's account.

Andrew again wondered if Jennifer could somehow have carried out this act of retribution while Roddy was at the concert with the boys, but he just couldn't believe it. She loved the club as much as he did, and would never do something like this. And why would she frame her son's best friend? Just the image of petite little Jennifer tearing around the greens on a tractor seemed laughable. But *someone* did it, God dammit! The thought still angered him, even now.

He patted his tie and stood tall before the mirror. Excellent. With a conscious commitment to push these thoughts from his mind, he strode out of the bedroom and down the stairs for breakfast.

"Morning, Mr. President," Mary greeted him with a kiss. "Ready for your big day?"

"Sure am, Hon." Andrew looked at the plates of French toast and sausages Cindy and Mike were already plowing through. A small bowl of grain cereal, a half-grapefruit and a little cocktail glass full of fresh blueberries waited for him at his own place setting.

"Looks like somebody is thinking about breaking their diet," Mary chided. "How 'bout a couple of sausage links for good luck today?"

"No, no," he protested. "They do smell great, but I don't want to start cheating again."

At that, Mary whirled away from him and returned to the sink. He instantly regretted his choice of words. Did she suspect something about Jennifer? He didn't think so, but changed the subject.

"You guys'd be impressed with your old man's presentation. I really dove into PowerPoint for this one. Instead of the usual ho-hum slides of financial tables and pie charts, I jazzed it up with some cool animations, pictures of the grounds and imbedded plots from Excel. It looks a lot more high-tech than my old ones. Maybe the board members will even pay attention."

"Cool, Dad," said Mike, sounding less than fully attentive.

Cindy sat feverishly texting on her phone, neither listening nor eating.

"You guys have to do that kind of thing for school?" Andrew asked. "And Pumpkin, no phones at the table, right?"

"It's about homework, Dad," Cindy answered without looking up. "Millie and Kate got different answers than me on our math thing for today."

Andrew decided to let it go. He mostly wanted any idle conversation to cover his "cheating" gaffe. He figured he was just being paranoid anyway.

The Ashland family finished their breakfast in disconnected silence. Mike and Cindy picked up their lunches and bookbags and drifted off to school. Mary collected the dirty dishes and gave him another kiss on the top of his head.

"Good luck today, Honey. I know you'll do well."

---

The afternoon crowd at the Sutter Valley clubhouse seemed a little lighter than usual, but that was fine with Andrew. Cheerful members and staff flowed throughout the lobby, bar and dining room. That's the image he hoped the board members would internalize. He politely exchanged greetings and handshakes with some of the regulars, but he wanted to go through his presentation one last time before the meeting.

Jennifer had already set things up in the conference room. He could feel the tension in his whole body relax when she looked up from the display controller with one of her smirks from the old days.

"Hey, Boss. Display screen's broken. You can just use sock puppets for this, right?"

"Yeah, no problem, Jen. Can you back me up on the banjo?" Until this moment, he hadn't realized how much he had stressed about Jennifer's support today, given the recent developments in their relationship.

"I'll just need a few minutes to tune up, but you got it."

"You're shittin' me, right? The thing's not really broken, is it?"

"It's working fine, Andrew. You're so damn gullible."

"All right, ya got me. I'd be so pissed if all the friggin' time I put into this slideshow was wasted. Can I plug in and go through a dry run?"

"Ready when you are." Jen handed him a cord and powered up the controller.

Like the rest of the clubhouse, no cash had been spared on the conference room. The chairs were plush but professional, placed around a U-shaped trio of beautifully finished tables. The back and side walls displayed pictures of various locations around the course, along with a few famous golfers and celebrities who had played at the club over the years. The focal point of the room, of course, was the gargantuan video screen that covered the entire front wall.

He cycled through the entire presentation. He had worried that the laser pointer/cursor that had come with the display system wouldn't connect with his laptop, but everything ran like clockwork. His slides looked even more impressive in large scale. Awesome. Now he'd have at least twenty minutes to loosen up with a scotch and hobnob with the board members at the bar before the meeting.

As expected, all of the board members had shown up early to take advantage of their open bar privileges before the meeting. Carl O'Brien, the most senior member of the board, looked as though he'd had quite a head start.

"You've had another great year, Andy-boy!" he slurred to Andrew from his barstool, spilling most of his drink on his sleeve while giving Andrew a pat on the shoulder.

"Thanks, Carl. You've been a big part of it yourself." Andrew answered, trying to engage almost anyone else in conversation.

"Andrew!" a voice to his right called.

"Father Ed! How are you?"

"Couldn't be better, Andrew. Glad to see the crew has already fixed up the green from last week. Terrible mess, that was."

"It certainly was, Father. I plan to address that very topic in the meeting. I don't expect we'll ever have to deal with that kind of trouble in the future."

"Glad to hear it. Oh, hello Silvia!" Father Ed turned to address Silvia Fentisco, who had tapped him on the shoulder.

Silvia and her husband George were both long-standing board members. They were also known as the biggest gossips in Sutter Valley. Mary once joked that revealing a "secret" to Silvia would be a quicker way to share it with the entire town than putting it on the evening news. Silvia's gossiping didn't bother Andrew that much, but her obnoxious New Jersey accent pierced through his skull like a drill. Again, Andrew found himself desperately looking for any friendly face in the crowd. He spotted Harold "Buck" Buxbey telling an apparently hilarious story to a few other board members by the big picture window. Bingo! Buck had been his closest friend since he and Mary had moved to Sutter Valley over fifteen years ago. He snatched his scotch from the bar with a nod to the bartender and beelined to the window.

"Hey, El Presidente!" Buck called out as Andrew joined their informal group. "Gonna show us some good numbers tonight?"

"I think you'll be very pleased, Buck, but don't think that means you can sleep through the presentation... again." Andrew smiled as the rest of the group sniggered at Buck's expense.

"Well, I just hope you covered your tracks better than last year with all the embezzling you've been doing." Buck laughed at his own joke, but a few people in the group looked uncomfortable; unsure if Andrew would take offense.

"I think I'm pretty well covered," Andrew answered with a big grin. "I did have to pay off our accountant, of course."

Buck chuckled along with the others, and returned to his epic tale about a home repair he and his son had made much worse by trying to fix it themselves. As always, his animated retelling of the whole disaster entertained everyone. He was just about to launch into another episode when Jennifer announced the meeting would begin in five minutes. The board members took the cue as a "last call," and rushed the bar for a final round.

Once everyone took their seats in the conference room and settled down, Andrew started the presentation. He panicked for a moment. When the screen first powered up, he could have sworn he saw the image of an orange-colored skull. What the hell? Maybe the logo of the company that made the computer screen? Thankfully the freakish image disappeared and the first slide of his presentation filled the screen. No one else seemed to notice.

"Thank you all for coming, distinguished members of the Sutter Valley Golf Club board. Tonight, I'd like to share our business results with you, but first I would like to take a moment to address the most recent and disturbing event that took place on Thursday night of last week."

He clicked his laser pen to show a slide of the horrendously damaged green, with the tractor left in its abandoned position.

"As you can see, someone broke into one of our maintenance sheds, took one of the tractors and badly damaged one of our most treasured greens." He clicked through slides of the shed door and a few more angles of the green damage. The board members shook their heads and murmured comments of disgust.

"Though we have not yet caught the person or persons responsible, rest assured that we have taken steps not only to repair the damage, but to ensure that this will never happen again. At least, not without severe legal consequences for the perpetrators."

He advanced through several more slides, showing the progressive repairs to the green, then to shots of the new security cameras, and finally to the new "security room" with the monitors and computers to support the new system. Andrew wondered if any of the veteran members would recognize the new "security headquarters" as the former overflow storage closet for the club bar.

"Finally, as the most important part of our new security measures, allow me to introduce Daniel Greene, of O.L. Security." He gestured to a youngish-looking guard, who had snuck in the back of the conference room during the presentation.

Daniel gave a shy wave, and a severely buzzed Carl started to clap. Others joined in, and Andy gestured again to Daniel. As the clapping ebbed, he gave a quick little bow and left the room to resume his duties.

"Hopefully these steps will assure you that the Sutter Valley Golf Club will never again fall victim to this kind of senseless destruction. As always, do not hesitate to let me know of any security concerns you feel have not been addressed by these actions, and you have my word that I will take immediate steps to ensure that our club property will be protected in the best possible way. Are there any questions?"

Seeing only nods of assent, Andrew pressed on. Jennifer, seated in one of the seats nearest to him, gave him an encouraging thumbs up. No one had asked about the cost. He had been prepared to take on that topic, had anyone asked, but everyone must have realized security was no longer a luxury item; it was a must-have.

"In much happier news, let's take a look at this year's financials."

So far, his professional looking slideshow had everyone engaged. The financial portion of the report would be the true test, though. Even the most attentive board members' eyes would start to glaze over during the monotonous financial analysis, and a few would fall asleep outright. Jen referred to them as the truly "bored" board members.

He clicked again to bring up a screen of the previous year's financials, which showed a lackluster return at the club bar, restaurant and course usage.

"I'm sure that you all recall the situation last year. Though club membership numbers had remained flat to slightly positive, sales at our restaurant and bar declined significantly." He used the cursor to superimpose a pair of downward trending plots on his financial plot of club funds.

"So I made two big changes at the start of the year. First, I hired a top-end chef." Another click; a face shot of the new head chef and culinary director. "I know you've all met Armand by now." A few scattered claps for Armand.

"Of course, this added additional operating cost, but our menu offerings more than tripled." Next slide, a comparison of the two menus – before and after Armand. Any fool could see that Armand's new menu totally kicked the ass of the old one. More nods and mumblings of agreement.

"The next big change was to require a two-hundred-dollar minimum monthly dining room fee to all members. We got a lot of push-back on this one. But let's take a look at the numbers." After only two months of, shall we say, a 'forced introduction' to our new menu offerings, we no longer had to require the minimum fee. In fact, our restaurant has become so popular that we now have a waiting list!

The next animation overlayed the current year's restaurant returns over the previous year's anemic plot. What a difference!

"And as we'd hoped, sales at the bar went hand-in-hand with the popularity of the dining room."

Andrew clicked the pen to show this year's bar sales plot also crushing the poor performance of the previous year. To his delight, aside from Carl, everyone looked attentive and pleased. Yes! Carl had completely passed out, but at least hadn't started snoring. His drink rose and fell as he breathed, balanced on his ample belly.

"Nice job, Mr. President!" Buck chimed in from the back, and another round of clapping broke out.

Andrew demurely shrugged and continued.

"What we *didn't* expect was the increase in both course usage and new memberships. The sharpest increase in fifteen years!

He clicked again, knowing this next animation was the coolest. It would show the final numbers for the year up until now, an unprecedented leap. The increased profit percentage would blow up with a balloon and fireworks graphic; the climax of the presentation. He turned his back on the screen to watch its effect on the board members. But instead of big smiles, he saw only confusion and wide-eyed shock. Jennifer looked absolutely horrified. He turned back to face the screen and immediately understood.

Unbelievably, the presentation had switched to a full-scale movie of Jennifer and him passionately making love in the lounge! The faces were unmistakable, and the video left nothing to the imagination. As the board members continued to watch, he madly pressed buttons on the laser pen to no effect. He couldn't move, or even breathe.

Jennifer dove on top of the screen controller and started frantically yanking cords. Still, the humiliating video played on. What the hell? The video switched to another location, where Jennifer was topless, astride Andrew on one of the couches in the main lounge. This was a disaster, and he was frozen like the proverbial deer in the headlights.

Sylvia Fentisco blurted "Oh my Gawwwd!" in her outrageous accent, and even Carl woke up to watch the excitement. Someone whistled and a few people snickered.

Some unseen smartass, imitating Buck's earlier comment, snorted "Nice job, Mr. President!"

Andrew stumbled his way around the chairs along the table and pulled the power cord to the display itself. The screen mercifully went blank, but only after showing the beginning of yet *another* wild tryst in Andrew's office. Jennifer covered her face, crying, and dashed out of the now darkened room.

Everyone looked at him, expecting some kind of explanation. What the hell could he possibly say? At the very least, this would cost him his job as president. Much worse, he would probably lose his wife and family. He couldn't fathom the sense of shame that he would feel; that they would *all* feel as word of his scandalous behavior cascaded through Sutter Valley.

He would need to race home to tell Mary and the kids before they heard it from someone else. Just the thought of that conversation shook him, and he collapsed on the front table, cradling his head in his hands.

The board members filed out, still in shock themselves. Buck stopped as he walked by, and placed his hand on Andrew's shoulder.

"Jesus Christ, Andrew. You and I both know this is gonna be tough. Just remember you've got a friend, here. Call me if there's anything I can do, OK?"

Andrew nodded and tried to collect himself. Buck patted him again and followed the others out of the conference room.

His whole body still shook, and he felt like he was moving outside himself, as though in a dream. Or nightmare, more accurately. How in God's name could this have happened? He knew he had no one to blame but himself for the affair, but who would have recorded him with Jennifer, and somehow worked it into his presentation? He even did a dry run through the slides, for Christ's sake! Whoever did it clearly wanted to expose him at his most vulnerable and most public moment. But who, and why? He'd had a few disagreements with club and even board members over the years, but nothing serious enough to deserve this kind of retribution. At least nothing he could remember. Then it hit him. Roddy! Either Jennifer must have told him, or he figured it out for himself. Shit! It had to be Roddy. Even at the cost of humiliating himself as the unwitting cuckhold, Roddy must have concocted the most devastating revenge scheme ever. And the bastard had pulled it off. Perfectly.

But his confrontation with Hot Rod would have to wait. He would probably wind up getting his ass kicked, on top of all else, but right now that concern seemed trivial. Walking like a condemned man to the gallows, he plodded down the hall to get his car keys. In a few minutes, he would have to begin the most painful conversation of his life.

## Chapter 10 - The Sixth Task: Dance Club Break-in

Three thousand dollars. On top of the nearly five thousand or so that he'd already collected from his previous Hoodlum shenanigans, Eddie supposed he now had enough to buy at least a halfway decent used car. Or a pretty sweet used road bike, if he could somehow convince his mother. But right now, thoughts of spending his fortune barely crossed his mind. He had picked up the task reward money yesterday afternoon, and had just read the next task assignment on the Hoodlum laptop.

He stared at the laptop screen, hoping he had somehow misread the details of the next challenge.

*TASK #6 REWARD: $3000*

**GREETINGS, HOODLUM!**

**TASK #6 WILL BE YOUR TOUGHEST CHALLENGE YET. IT'S TIME TO STEP OUTSIDE OF**

SHELTERED LITTLE SUTTER VALLEY -- TIME TO REALLY PUSH YOURSELF!

FOR THIS TASK, YOU MUST BREAK INTO THE 'HELLO DOLLY' GENTLEMAN'S CLUB IN KENDALL'S CORNERS. ONCE INSIDE, YOU WILL NEED TO ENTER THE BUSINESS OFFICE AND STEAL A SINGLE FILE FROM THE RECORDS CABINET. YOUR OBJECTIVE IS THE FOLDER LABELED "EMPLOYEE TAX WITHHOLDING FOR 1994."

THE IDEAL TIME TO COMPLETE THIS TASK IS BETWEEN 10PM AND 6AM THIS SUNDAY/MONDAY, WHEN THE CLUB CLOSES EARLY.

AS BEFORE, YOU WILL NEED TO PICK UP A PACKAGE OF SUPPLIES AND ADDITIONAL INSTRUCTIONS AT THE USUAL SPOT.

YOU HAVE PROVEN YOURSELF WORTHY AND RESOURCEFUL SO FAR. REMEMBER, AFTER TASK #7, ALL WILL BE REVEALED. KEEP THE FAITH -- YOU ARE ALMOST THERE!

AS ALWAYS, GOOD LUCK, HOODLUM!

KIND REGARDS,

*THE HOODLUM GAMEMASTER*

One hell of a way to start a Saturday morning. He had first awakened with happy but nervous thoughts of his date with Emma later on. Even those thoughts now slipped away from him as he tried to envision breaking into the Hello Dolly strip club. Eddie had never been inside the place, but it was well known to every high school boy by reputation alone. A bold few even claimed to have snuck inside for "the show," though their stories always sounded made up.

The club was located about six miles away in a little town called Kendall's Corners. More of an intersection than a town, Kendall's Corners included a handful of houses, a liquor store, a drug store, a diner and of course, the "Hello Dolly Gentleman's Club." If you passed through town, the "Dolly" was impossible to miss. The other businesses and homes looked grey and uninteresting, but not the Dolly! A massive neon sign featured a buxom blonde, alternately standing in an innocent pose, then bending over in her short shorts, boobs nearly bursting out of her tank top. He and his mother would both pretend to ignore the place whenever they drove by it on their way to the lake. She would usually make a joke about how small the town was, saying the zip code started with a decimal point, or something similar. And if she said nothing, Eddie would feel obligated to say something, really *anything* to avert the awkwardness of driving past a neon-boobed strip club with his mom.

But remembering those uncomfortable moments didn't hold a candle to the feelings he had about the Hello Dolly right now. He could picture Mike, leaning against the garage wall with an I-told-you-so expression. The whole Hoodlum mess had played out exactly as Mike had prophesized, and Eddie had no choice but to continue even further down this dark path.

Eddie thought about quitting. The Gamemaster had already shown him the consequences. He would have to own up to all of the crimes he had committed, and would have to pay the price. He could forget about college scholarships for certain, and probably even college at all. His shot at the military would disappear, and he may not even get to finish high school. His mother would have to spend what little money they had on legal fees. Worst of all, he would be selling Mike out, too. The thought of his own life falling apart was bad enough, but to rob such a promising and popular kid like Mike of his future seemed unthinkable. Quitting was not an option. He would have to go through with it.

But how? Just getting to the club would be a problem. Kendall's Corners seemed too far of a ride for the bike at night. He could risk taking the car, and hope that his mother wouldn't wake up. On any other night of the week, he could have told her he would be working late at the store. She knew Silver's closed early on Sundays, though. Maybe he could tell her he had another date with Emma? That might work.

But getting there and back represented only a minor part of the challenge. Even though his criminal portfolio now included breaking into the private residence of a cop, he would be utterly out of his element on this one. The Gamemaster had covered him pretty well last time, but it had still been a close call. What if the club owner happened to linger after hours? How could the

Gamemaster control something like that? Beyond just getting caught, he might get clubbed with a bat or have his head blown off with a shotgun. This wasn't the cozy residential community he knew; this was the real deal -- breaking into a business with ample experience handling unruly drunks and lowlife characters. The security system probably included cameras and God knows what else the Gamemaster could have overlooked. Eddie started to tremble, just thinking of all the ways this could go wrong. He pictured himself in the back of a squad car, hiding his head in shame while his mother wept for his worthless soul.

And for what? He had already given up on trying to solve the mystery of the game. He had no idea what could possibly link all of these apparently pointless tasks together. USB thumb drives, stolen mermaids, vandalized road signs, ruined golf courses, framed classmates and now some obscure tax forms from a strip club – it made less sense now than ever. He didn't need any more cash, either. Hell, he couldn't even figure out a way to explain or spend the money he'd already earned!

Eddie felt stupid, and imagined watching himself as the clueless victim on some reality prank show. And he knew that he'd be in this same hopeless predicament for whatever evil deed that task number seven held in store. If that was really going to be the final task, as the Gamemaster promised.

Eddie slammed the laptop closed and stuffed it back into its hiding place in the garage cupboard. If he picked up the task six supply package right now, he could focus on the much happier matter of his date with Emma. He jogged across the backyard and through the woods, wondering how many more times he'd have to do this.

Just as he reached the pickup spot a good-sized bass blasted out of the water, snatching some unlucky bug for a snack. Not many more fishing days left this season, Eddie pined. He took a thoughtful look around his peaceful little pond. So much had happened since the day he'd found the Hoodlum laptop. Was that only two weeks ago?

The top edge of the Hoodlum envelope stuck just far enough out of the grass to be seen by someone looking for it. A smaller envelope sat tucked Inside the large envelope. It held two keys; a large official looking one that probably opened the main door, and a smaller one he assumed would open either the business office or the file cabinet inside the office.

He pulled out some papers, which included a floorplan of the main floor, a picture of the security keypad and a list of codes, a diagram of the parking lot and security cameras, and another small paragraph of instructions. Pretty much what he expected. He stuffed the contents back in the envelope and did his best to push the task from his mind for the rest of the day.

---

If Eddie had worried about what to wear for the big date, he would have wasted his time. His mother had already set out his "dress up" jeans, and now stood in his closet agonizing over his meager selection of decent shirts.

"We really need to get you some nicer clothes, Eddie Bear. Not just for dates, but for college interviews and graduation parties and things." She shook her head and put two shirts she'd been comparing back in the closet.

"I got some nice shirts for work," Eddie offered. "Won't get me on the cover of GQ, but good enough for Silver's." He struck an exaggerated modeling pose, hoping to get his mom to laugh.

Tina sighed and swept her hand once more across the drab row of hanging shirts.

"Hey," she sounded hopeful. "How 'bout this one?"

Eddie never would have chosen the shirt she picked out. She had given it to him as a birthday gift last year, and he had only worn it once. It was a short-sleeved button-down shirt with brightly colored squares of different sizes. At the time he thought the colors were a little too flashy, but now it looked like his best option.

When his mother had first asked him what he planned to wear for the big date, he'd panicked. He worried about dressing too fancy, not fancy enough, too weird, too dorky, too childish… you name it. And who knew what Emma would wear? Jesus, could this be any more stressful?

He was too embarrassed to ask for her advice, but his stunned expression had been invitation enough.

"Perfect, Mom. Thanks."

She held the shirt up in front of him and looked like she was about to cry.

---

At precisely five o'clock, Eddie rounded the corner onto Emma's street. Her neighborhood wasn't part of the central Sutter Valley Community; it was one of several residential streets between the golf course and the school. To Eddie, the homes here looked less pretentious than many of the larger homes around his neighborhood.

He had ridden by Emma's house on his bike yesterday to check it out. Her house reminded him of his own, though the yard and landscaping looked much nicer. A Subaru with a pair of kayaks on its rack sat in the driveway. It looked like Emma's family enjoyed the outdoors...maybe even fishing?

The Subaru was in the driveway again today, but the kayaks were gone. He pulled his car right behind it and started to climb out. As he did, he noticed that his mother must have gotten the car washed. Wow, she thought of everything!

He had kind of wanted to meet Emma's parents, but felt relieved when Emma just popped her head out the front door, waved goodbye to her folks and dashed out to the car. If things went well, as he hoped, he would meet them soon enough. Someone had pulled the curtains aside to peek out the window at him, but he couldn't tell who it was.

Eddie had to scramble to get around the car quickly enough to open the passenger door for Emma. When she realized he planned to open her door for her, she responded by acting like pompous royalty. The gesture made Eddie laugh and put him right at ease. It struck him how much Emma reminded him of his mother.

"Hey Emma – you look great!" Eddie slid back into the driver seat. She sported jeans and a cute but casual looking blouse. Just right.

"You too, Eddie. That's a really cool shirt."

"Thanks. My mom picked it out," he confessed. "She was almost as nervous about tonight as I was." Eddie hadn't planned to reveal all of this, but he felt a strange compulsion to be truthful with Emma.

"Aw, that's so cute! This is the first time I've gone out on a real date, and my dad wanted to meet you and have a serious talk about 'the rules,'" Emma air quoted. "He's really not mean or intimidating at all. My mom talked him out of it. It was sweet, though. I know he was just being protective."

Eddie turned the car onto the main road and drove towards the little plaza about a mile past the high school. Dalton Plaza featured a pizza place, an ice cream shop, a mini golf course, a burger joint, a specialty store for exotic pets and the only movie theater within at least ten miles. Everyone knew that the Dalton Plaza was the cultural hub of the Sutter Valley Community.

"This is your first date, too?" Eddie asked.

"First date ever! How am I doing so far?"

"Well, I guess we'll see. You have your first big decision coming up already."

"Wow! That's a lot of pressure for so early in the date. What's the big decision?"

"Here it is -- you ready?"

Emma nodded and pressed her index fingers on her temples, feigning intense concentration.

"So, I looked at the extensive list of movie offerings at our local cinema," he said. "All both of them."

"And?" asked Emma.

"A very disappointing selection. A choice between one of the never-ending Jason: Friday the 13th sequels, or an animated kids' movie. And I'm gonna guess that you aren't a big 'Jason' fan."

"Good guess," she answered. "I watched the first one and had nightmares for weeks."

"That's good news. So here's your big decision. How 'bout instead of a movie, we play Mini Golf, and then get pizza or burgers for dinner?"

"If that's my big decision, I'm rockin' this. That sounds like a perfect plan to me!"

"Nice work, Emma. You are crushing this date thing so far. Are you good at Mini Golf?"

"Funny you should ask. I'm actually planning to go to college on a Mini Golf scholarship."

"Really?" he asked, turning to look at her. Was she joking? She looked totally serious...for a moment.

"I'm just kidding, Eddie," she laughed. "I've played a few times, but that's it. I can beat my dad, but I'm pretty sure he lets me win. Are you a big golf pro?"

"I'm pretty bad, but it's kinda fun. I can't tell if my mom lets me win, or if she's actually even worse than me."

Eddie parked right in front of the Lumberjack Mini Golf course lot and flew around the back of the car to open Emma's door. She smirked as she climbed out of the car, then strutted as though she was a Hollywood celebrity on her way down the red carpet. Eddie had to laugh as she primly offered her hand for him to escort her. He still worried that he might say something stupid, but he felt so much more relaxed with Emma than he expected. Certainly more than he would with any other girl.

The Hoodlum Game

"Two of ya, eh?" growled the old woman that always managed the Lumberjack golf course.

To Eddie, she seemed eternally tired and grouchy. He remembered an embarrassing moment a few years back when the old lady busted his mom doing an imitation of her. She sighed heavily, then slowly rose from her chair and gave them each a putter and matching golf ball.

"Thank you so much!" said Emma cheerily. The grumpy old woman had already plodded halfway back to her rocker, but even she was not immune to Emma's good nature. She turned to look at Emma and Eddie more closely and smiled through missing teeth.

"You kids have a good time now, y' hear?"

Emma started right off the bat with a hole in one. She tried not to laugh at Eddie's three failed attempts at the same hole, then cheered when he finally sunk the putt.

Emma continued to whup Eddie for the next few holes. Eddie didn't enjoy losing so badly, but he was having such a good time that it didn't bother him.

"So," he said after she sank yet another long putt. "Where is this Mini Golf college you'll be attending? Do they offer remedial putting instruction for the less gifted, or do they cater exclusively to the pros?"

"Oh, I'm afraid it's pros only at Mini Golf U. At least in the scholarship program. In fact, we're not to even *associate* with golfers that can't meet par."

Eddie drooped his head in mock despair.

"Awww, don't worry," Emma patted his shoulder supportively. "I'm sure they offer programs in putting green maintenance, lumberjack sculpting and mini-windmill repair. There's a place for *everyone* at Mini Golf U!"

Eddie laughed and took another swing, sending his ball past the hole and down an incline; now even further away than before.

"Even me?" he asked.

Emma cringed at his last shot finally rolled to a stop. "You may need to supplement your application with a sizeable donation, but I'm sure there's a place for you."

"That's very comforting to hear." Eddie finally sank the putt, and they moved on to the next hole.

This was so much better than going to the movies. He had worried that he might run out of things to talk about, but Emma followed his mild sarcasm and humorous comments like a natural. She even threw in some zingers herself. And she looked so damn cute! Though she seemed at ease conversationally, her quirky movements reminded him of a frightened cat. To Eddie, her nervousness just added to her cuteness and vulnerability.

The next several holes treated Eddie less cruelly, but he had no chance of catching up to Emma. At the second to last hole, she skillfully putted past the main feature obstacle; a giant Paul Bunyan-sized lumberjack whose axeblade swished back and forth across a narrow opening between his huge lumberjack boots. Emma had timed her shot perfectly. Her ball passed easily between the axeblade strokes through a little chute to the green beyond. They peeked around the obstacle and watched her ball stop just a few inches short of the hole. Eddie slumped in defeat while Emma took a dramatic bow for her performance.

For Eddie's turn, he squarely hit the swinging axeblade, which sent his ball right back to the starting point. Emma giggled, and he turned around to give her the snobbish "quiet on the course" gesture. He took a second whack and the same exact thing happened. Emma snickered again and he repeated the all-quiet gesture, though he was now laughing himself. When his third shot again hit the blade obstacle directly in the center, Emma completely lost it. She doubled over in hysterics while Eddie stomped forward to just kick his ball past the unyielding axe.

As he kicked it, the ball jammed hard directly beneath the axe blade, abruptly stopping its movement. The familiar swishing motor noise changed to a distressed grinding sound. Emma was convulsed. Eddie couldn't knock the ball free with the putter, and the grinding grew louder. He could smell something burning, and smoke began to billow out from behind the giant Paul Bunyan. He grabbed the axe itself, but it wouldn't budge. The grinding sound became a loud whine, and both he and Emma laughed uncontrollably. He finally kicked the wooden axe blade, and his ball shot through the obstacle to join Emma's on the far side. Mercifully, the axe motor stopped whining, but a cloud of smoke continued to spew forth. The axe blade hung motionless between Paul Bunyan's boots, now blocking the narrow opening forever.

Eddie took a quick look around. Luckily, they were the only people on this part of the course. They hadn't really done anything wrong, but he didn't want to incur the wrath of the old woman that ran the place. He had tears in his eyes from laughing so hard.

Between peals of laughter, Emma pointed at the lumberjack and howled, "It looks like Mr. Bunyan is suffering from a little gastric distress!"

From this angle, it looked as though the smoke was blasting right out of the giant lumberjack's ass. This observation started them both laughing hysterically all over again. Eddie could not remember the last time he had laughed so hard. Definitely not since the Hoodlum ordeal began.

They continued to rekindle each other's laughing fits during the last hole, and even Emma had to take several shots to sink her final putt. They turned in their putters and strolled towards the restaurant. Eddie took Emma's hand. She squeezed back and playfully bumped his shoulder as they walked along. She seemed to be enjoying herself as much as he was.

"Well, Emma, I sure hope your lack of respect for mini golf obstacles doesn't jeopardize your big scholarship."

"Hopefully they'll never find out. I don't see any police cars or helicopters yet, so maybe we got away with our big crime."

"I think you're right," Eddie said. "We should probably continue to surveil the area from a nearby restaurant just to be sure, though. Whattaya think? Burger place or pizza?"

"Wow, tough call. The burger place has a better view of the crime scene, but we'd also be more exposed. The pizza place is more concealed, and they have a door on the far side if we need to escape," she reasoned. "Besides, I just had a burger for dinner last night."

"Great call. Pizza it is."

They walked past the outdoor seating area of "Beefy Blue's" burger restaurant and up the walkway to "Pizazz's Pizza Parlor." Though it was still early, several families and couples already occupied tables at both places. An elderly couple turned to watch them, perhaps nostalgically remembering their own dating days.

Eddie had eaten at both restaurants many times, but had never once imagined himself strolling hand in hand on a date to either one. The thought made him feel very mature.

---

The sun had set over two hours ago, but the sky still hadn't darkened enough for Eddie's liking. He crouched in clustered scrub brush behind a pair of dumpsters. The dumpsters sat across the parking lot from the rear kitchen door of "Hello Dolly" strip club. To add to his discomfort, the godawful smell of grease and garbage from the dumpsters nauseated him to the pit of his stomach. He tried to breathe only through his mouth, but that didn't help much. More than anything, Eddie just wanted to put this task behind him.

The club's Sunday evening crowd had already started to dwindle. Only a few cars, two trucks and three motorcycles remained in the parking lot -- at least as far as he could see. From this angle he couldn't tell if anyone had parked directly in front of the place.

To solve his transportation problem, he had borrowed a moped from Steve Kagasimi. When Emma agreed to the date, he gave Steve his Saturday evening shift back again. Just by chance, Steve mentioned that his mother had bought a moped but never used it. He told Eddie she wouldn't miss the lame thing if he took it for a month.

Though he felt foolish riding the bright orange underpowered bike, it greatly simplified getting to and from Kendall's Corners. On top of that, it easily stored inside the backyard shed. When his mother had gone upstairs, he pedaled it down the street before starting the engine. She didn't hear a thing. That part of the plan had worked out surprisingly well.

Like last time, he had taken the time to check out the satellite view of the area on the internet. The Kendall's Corners liquor store parking lot butted right up against the Hello Dolly lot. Right now, the moped stood alone in the otherwise vacant liquor store lot. He had parked it to avoid visibility from the strip club, but a row of streetlamps covered the rear border of both parking lots. To Eddie, the moped stood out like a sore thumb, but hopefully the strip club crowd wouldn't notice.

On the plus side, the Gamemaster's diagram of lights and security cameras perfectly matched what Eddie could now see with his own eyes. That thought gave him some small comfort as he waited for the Dolly to close.

Occasionally someone would step out the kitchen door to smoke a cigarette. He had one scare shortly after he first arrived. A kitchen worker blasted through the door with garbage bags and strode right up to the dumpsters to toss them in. Eddie had dropped low, but at that point the darkness couldn't conceal him at all. Luckily, the guy didn't even glance beyond the dumpsters. Apart from that near miss, things had stayed relatively quiet. He could hear muffled dance music from inside the club, periodically interrupted by the announcer's voice and scattered applause.

Naturally, Eddie was curious about the show and would have loved to see inside for himself. He'd caught a glimpse of one of the dancers walking in from the parking lot earlier, and she looked like a bombshell. At least she did from behind the dumpsters in semi-darkness. As closing time drew near, though, worrying about getting caught shifted his focus from such distractions. But since he still had almost another full hour to wait, he did allow his thoughts to turn back to his date with Emma the night before.

He'd enjoyed his dinner at Pizazz's Pizza even more than the Mini Golf. The pizza itself had been OK, but he'd barely tasted it. They had asked each other questions about their families, favorite movies, pet peeves, dream vacation spots, college and career plans, the works. He learned that Emma had a little brother and that her family did love the outdoors. She had only tried fishing once or twice, though, and didn't remember much about it. For the most part Emma's interests matched well with his own. He had to admit a twinge of disappointment that she didn't share the love that Eddie and his mother had for Chinese food, but everything else seemed to fit so well that it really didn't matter. He supposed they should differ on at least a few things, anyway.

Though Eddie would protest when his mother picked a romantic movie for them to watch together, he always paid careful attention to how the "ideal guy" should behave on a date. When he thought about it, most things seemed obvious – asking questions about the girl's interests and opinions, avoiding jabbering on endlessly about his own, being kind to others, not just to her, acting like a gentleman, and really listening to what she says. Reflecting on their date, he believed he had done all of those things quite well.

Even so, he worried about scaring her off by moving too quickly. And by "moving too quickly" he didn't mean making grabby sexual advances; he wouldn't do that to Emma. He simply didn't want to creep her out by coming on too strong.

He was conscious of his own naivety, but he already wondered if Emma could be the one and only girl for him. Hopefully she felt the same way, but he didn't really know. He could only hope that his infatuation wasn't obvious. Could others see his puppy-like adoration of her? If his true feelings for Emma did show, he had no idea how to suppress it.

The kitchen door banged open again, jarring him from his thoughts. This time he could see and sort of hear an old guy, maybe a cook, and a younger guy talking and smoking. Could this mean the end of the shift was near? Once he convinced himself that they weren't about to walk out to the dumpster, Eddie relaxed. His mind drifted once again to his date with Emma.

They both had such a great time talking and joking at dinner that neither one of them wanted the date to end. Since Eddie had insisted on paying for Mini Golf and dinner, Emma suggested milkshakes for dessert – but only if he would let her pay. Eddie happily accepted, so they switched restaurants and spent the next hour talking about kids at school and their jobs at Silver's. When Emma mentioned how nice Eric Silver seemed, Eddie shared his hopes to somehow get Eric and his mother together.

"Oh, that would be fantastic!" Emma had said. "I know I haven't even met your mom yet, but I can just imagine what a perfect couple they'd be!"

"I think so, too." It hadn't occurred to Eddie until that moment how helpful Emma could be in coordinating his big meet-up scheme. "She already agreed to have a cookout for my friends from Silver's," he said. "Of course I would invite Eric, too, so they would sort of pair up naturally."

"Great idea. Neither one will suspect a thing. Now we just need to pick a time when we can get as many people from the store as possible – including Eric."

Eddie hadn't thought of that. He couldn't simply invite everyone from the store for a picnic dinner at once; Silvers was *always* open during dinnertime. And if Eddie invited even half of the usual workers to the picnic, Eric would probably insist on staying behind to help run the store.

"Good point," he said. "Any ideas for how we can do that?"

"Hmmmmm," Emma offered. "Let me work on that. I'll come up with something."

Eddie wondered if the picnic BBQ might also be the ideal opportunity to have him and his mother meet Emma's parents. And the fact that Emma said she'd "work on it" told Eddie that she hoped to spend more time with Eddie, too. Again, he didn't want to push things too quickly, yet everything seemed to be falling into place so perfectly. If only this damn Hoodlum thing was finished!

The muffled tunes from inside the "Dolly" had stopped. A few patrons ambled through the back door, lighting cigarettes and drifting towards pickups and street bikes. Within a few minutes the parking lot had nearly emptied. Two skinny looking guys remained, along with a girl in an unbelievably short skirt – obviously one of the dancers. Eddie couldn't hear the conversation, but it sounded like they planned to continue their party elsewhere. While they puffed and jabbered on, Eddie recalled the most epic moment of the date: his first kiss.

They both sat in the car outside Emma's house, still talking and laughing. Emma seemed to enjoy their time together as much as he did. A part of him had worried that she'd agreed to date him just to be "nice," which would have been typical of her. But the way she casually joked with him, fake-punched him, easily took his hand and returned his squeezes told him that she felt the same way.

He could barely believe it himself, but when she finally said goodnight, he boldly leaned right in and kissed her! Right on the lips! Emma had looked surprised, but hadn't pulled away. He immediately felt awkward, like it had been too spastic. He started to back off and apologize, but she gently placed her hand behind his neck and kissed him right back! This time he got it right. He hoped that her parents weren't watching out the window, but the electrifying sensation of the kiss was so overwhelming that he didn't really care. He guessed that most kids his age probably had this experience years earlier, but that thought took nothing away from the magic of the moment. And he could sense the same intense passion from Emma, too. They both sat breathless for a moment, then Emma took his hand.

"I had such a great time tonight, Eddie. Thank you so much for everything. I do hope you'll work on your Mini Golf skills, though. I'm really worried about your future."

My God, her smile. He loved the fact that even though she had such a kind and caring heart, she shared his edgy sense of humor.

"Me too, Emma. I had an awesome time, and I hope we can do it again soon. And I promise I'll work on my putting." His voice felt strange, and he felt as though every nerve in his body still vibrated from their long kiss. Did that really just happen? Even now, the whole date felt like a dream.

The last two bikes finally roared out of the parking lot, startling Eddie from his pleasant memory. The dancer hung on the back of one of the bikes; no helmet, hair billowing out behind her like a flag, fluttering short skirt covering very little at all.

Was the place finally closed? Though not well lit to begin with, Eddie had expected to see more lights turn off inside. The back and side lots now looked completely vacant, but what about the front? He didn't want to repeat the mistake he'd made during his careless exit from the Blackmoores' house. Eddie decided to back out from his location, walk around the far side of the liquor store, then look across both front lots to see if any cars remained.

To prevent the Gamemaster from getting any additional video of him committing crimes, Eddie had once again worn a facemask. This new one fit more comfortably and provided a much clearer view than his old one. He pulled it over his head and slipped around the back side of the liquor store. The main drag of Kendall's Corners was illuminated by only a few streetlamps, but that was enough to show Eddie that the front lot of the Dolly now stood empty. The big-boobed neon sign had been turned off, but several beer signs inside the windows still cast their own neon glow. Additional lighting seemed to emanate from unknown sources inside. To Eddie, the place looked about the same now as it did when it was open. He couldn't decide if that made him feel better or worse.

Eddie retraced his steps around the far side of the liquor store to his hiding spot behind the dumpsters. This was it – go time! Once again, the paralyzing feeling of dread overtook him. The images of himself locked in the back of a squad car, or getting beaten to a pulp in some backroom of the Dolly filled his head.

He had to get started, though. Even if this task went quickly, he'd be getting home crazy late. He adjusted his mask and started towards the rear customer entrance, per the Hoodlum instructions. By staying close to the building, he avoided the high camera over the door's entrance.

Even up close, he could not see through the dark glass door. The glass had some kind of opaque layer on the inside. He hoped to God that the place was truly empty, and punched the code into the security system. The alarm box was bigger than the Blackmoore's and the Ashford's, probably the commercial model, but it was also made by O.L.Security. Coincidence?

Eddie was rewarded with a soft double-beep and an "Alarm Deactivated" message on the screen. He stuck the big key in the door, opened it, and ducked inside. The walls, counters and tables stood jet black in the darkness, but dim lighting from the bar and stage area provided enough light for him to safely move around. He started to make his way to the business office, but took a moment to check out the stage and the famous stripper pole. He'd seen the setup many times in movies, but wondered what it must be like to see a live show. He walked past the DJ booth and down a narrow hallway to the business office, taking time to ogle the framed playbills that lined the hallway. The playbills looked like advertisements from the past, featuring nude and nearly nude starlets. A few of them looked cute, but he thought most just looked sleazy. Nothing at all like his Emma.

He could see double doors that led to the kitchen at the end of the hallway. As his eyes adjusted, he realized the waitress access to the bar was right next to him. He thought about grabbing himself a beer for later, but then decided he better just get on with it. Things had worked out so far; no need to push his luck. He continued down the hall. The second key unlocked the office door, and again there was just enough ambient light to move around without tripping over anything.

He saw a huge shadow move across the wall as he entered, and panicked. After a moment, he realized that the shadow was from an immense lighted aquarium along the back wall of the office. A weird bulgy-eyed fish swam in front of the light, casting strange shadows all around the room. Eddie calmed himself down and felt his way along the edge of a long desk to where the file cabinet should be. Sure enough, the Gamemaster had come through once again. He opened the cabinet and pulled out his mini mag light to read the folders. To his annoyance, the folders were completely out of order. Jesus, finding the right one could take forever. 1994 was almost 18 years ago. What if they didn't even have that file anymore? He wasn't seeing anything before 2005. Great. If he had gone through all this for nothing...

He tried the lower drawer. Sure enough, quite a few older folders down here, but again in no order whatsoever. After another minute or two of looking through the second drawer he found it - Employee Tax Withholding for 1994. Finally!

He clutched the folder and stood to leave. As he straightened up, he heard tires crunching through gravel and saw headlights sweep across the hall outside the office. Someone had just pulled into the lot directly in front of the Dolly! Sounded like at least one motorcycle, probably two. Holy shit! He could feel his stomach tighten. Had he tripped some alarm the Gamemaster hadn't mentioned?

He forced himself to slow down and think. Anyone who came in here after closing time was probably a manager and would almost certainly enter the office. He couldn't stay here. He figured the kitchen was his best bet. The kitchen was in the opposite direction from whoever was coming in, and it had its own exit to the back lot. He needed to get there quickly, though, otherwise whoever was coming in would catch him in the hallway.

Moving carefully, he closed the office door behind him. He could hear someone unlocking the front door, but at least they were still outside. Holding the folder close to his body, he took long strides down the hall to the kitchen. Several lights turned on just as he got to the door, but it didn't sound like anyone had made it to the hallway yet. He slipped as quietly as he could between the swinging doors to the kitchen.

He turned and stopped to listen. He could hear three distinct voices, and felt certain that they were the same two guys and girl that had lingered in the back lot after closing. From what he could hear, the girl had left her phone behind.

He could see more lights turning on through the gap in the door. Footsteps of at least one person walking down the hallway. The nerves of his spine tightened as the footsteps approached. The kitchen behind him offered no light whatsoever. He reached into his pocket for the mag light. Shit! He never picked it up after he grabbed the folder. If anyone entered the office, they would easily spot it, still brightly lit. Goddamn it – how stupid!

"What the hell?" someone shouted from the hallway. "I'm sure as shit that I locked the office. Alex, did you unlock this?"

"No, man," came a voice from further away, possibly near the bar. "I left 'fore you did, 'member? You went back for your smokes."

Eddie could hear the first guy stomping around inside the office.

"Dude, somebody has definitely been in here. File drawer is open and there's a flashlight on my desk!"

Eddie stood paralyzed. The second voice sounded much closer now.

"You sure? Did you check the safe?"

"Yes, I'm fuckin' sure! I mighta' left the door unlocked, but I sure as shit didn't leave a lit flashlight, dumbass. Safe's closed, but the file cabinet's open. Someone was definitely in here. We only been gone fifteen minutes. They're probly still here!"

Eddie needed no further prompting. Total darkness or not, he needed to get out now. He knew generally where the kitchen back door must be, so he stuck his arms out in front of him and walked in that direction. As he got closer, he could see light from the rear parking lot through the kitchen door window. Thank God! Eddie dropped his hands and moved directly for the door. As soon as he did, he felt his arm bump something. A second later, a metal tray clanged loudly on the floor.

"Kitchen! They're in the kitchen!"

He could hear at least one set of feet running towards him and the girl shouting to ask what was going on. He groped his way to the door and fumbled with the deadbolt. His hands were shaking so badly that he could barely work it, and he nearly dropped the damn folder. He fully expected the alarm to sound when he opened the door, but then realized the returning manager must have disabled it. Not that it mattered now.

He ran behind the dumpsters, then even further straight back through the thick woods behind the lot. Branches, thorns and briars stung and scraped him as he blundered his way through the brush. One particularly sharp branch jabbed him above the nose, narrowly missing his eye. He clutched the folder tightly. If he did somehow get away uncaught, but lost the folder, he knew he would never be bold enough to try this again. When he got deep enough in where the lights didn't penetrate, he finally dared to look back at the Dolly.

Eddie heard the kitchen door open. One of the skinny guys stepped outside, holding a bat and trying to look threatening. The other guy stuck his head out too, but after a moment they both went back inside. It occurred to Eddie that they might think that whoever broke in could have a weapon, so they were scared, too. They probably didn't feel like chasing somebody through the thick brush, and may not even realize which way he ran. Would they call the police? He hoped they hadn't noticed the moped behind the liquor store. The damn thing stood out like a homing beacon; its bright orange frame reflecting every photon from the parking lot lights. He wished he had stashed the moped in the woods somewhere further along the road toward home. Too late to worry about that now, though. All he could do was wait.

After another ten minutes had passed, he heard the street bikes start up again. That was a good sign – that meant they probably hadn't called the cops. Could it be a trick? He wondered if they would just wait a short way down the road for him to make a run for it. He almost laughed at the thought of trying to outrun a real street bike with the stupid moped. To his relief, both bikes tore off down the road towards the lake. Cool! Home was the other way, so he should be fine. He watched the tail lights fade into the distance before emerging from his hiding spot.

To add to his enjoyment, it had started to rain. Eddie tucked the folder under his shirt and jumped on the moped. Mindful of the fact that he could still be on camera, he decided to leave his mask on until he had put this dismal town in his rearview mirror.

Though he felt pretty confident that he'd gotten away with it, he couldn't help but check for headlights behind him every few seconds. Thankfully, he did not see traffic of any kind the whole way home. The trip took only fifteen minutes, but it felt like an hour. He thought of Emma as he passed Silver's, looking eerie and dead with its usual bright lights turned mostly off. He hoped Emma would never hear about any of his Hoodlum deeds. He couldn't even imagine her reaction.

When he finally got back to his street, he killed the engine and pedaled to his driveway, then around the garage to the backyard shed. Another nutball challenge in the bag.

This time more than any other, he wondered how the Gamemaster would ever know that he had stolen the folder. The previous two capers involved computers and could probably be verified by anyone with decent hacker skills, but this challenge involved the theft of a hard copy item. Would the Gamemaster ultimately ask for the folder itself as proof?

There must be some reason that he was directed to steal this specific file, of all things. If it was a piece of information that the Gamemaster needed, it could be a clue to his identity. Eddie realized it could also just be more misdirection; another meaningless mission with no rhyme nor reason whatsoever. But what if it wasn't? In any case, he knew he would need to take a good look at the contents of the folder.

He stepped through the door to the garage and pulled the chain on the small overhead light. Chances are that everyone in the neighborhood was sound asleep this late on a Sunday, but he didn't want to risk turning on the big overhead lights, just in case.

As expected, the folder contained income tax withholding forms for all of the employees at the Dolly for 1994. Nothing special; no Golden Ticket, no Holy Grail, no big clue that explained the whole damn Hoodlum game. He quickly flipped through the papers, about twenty or so in all.

Just as he was about to give up on finding any meaning at all in the ancient folder, he saw it. Second to last of the forms. Eddie read and re-read the name on the top of the tax form: Tina Ponzino. Comprehension hit him like a bucket of ice water poured over his head. According to these tax records, his own mother worked at the Hello Dolly strip club in 1994.

# Chapter 11 - End Game Preparations

Mondays were never Eddie's favorite day of the week, but this Monday felt much worse than any he could remember. Getting only a couple hours of sleep certainly contributed to the crappiness of the day. He struggled just to keep his eyes open during the Physics lecture. The teacher would probably notice, but there wasn't much Eddie could do about it. He could barely follow the discussion at all, and not just because he felt tired.

He did feel some relief for having completed his most daring Hoodlum crime yet, but the aftermath confused and disturbed him. The news that his mother had worked at the strip club had taken him utterly by surprise. He needed to confirm that it wasn't just coincidence. Ponzino wasn't a common name, but it wasn't exactly uncommon, either. He had checked the social security number against the card in her wallet this morning. It matched perfectly. What the hell?

Since then, his head swam with possible scenarios. Had she really been a dancer there, or maybe just a waitress or kitchen worker? After all, the tax folder included *all* employees, not just the dancers. When he thought about it, he decided that it didn't really bother him that she might have been a dancer. He didn't want anyone at school to find out, but beyond that he didn't feel any great shame. The thought of his mother actually "performing" made him uncomfortable, but he supposed that was natural. Admittedly, he had recently done quite a few things himself that he wasn't very proud of.

What *did* bother him was that she'd told him that she had moved away from her father in Georgia to come to this area in 1996, when he was a baby. Because of that, Eddie had always assumed that his own father was from Georgia, too. But these tax records showed her working here at least one year before Eddie was born. If that was true, then maybe his father was from around here.

Eddie had long understood that she felt embarrassed about her past, and he had never pressed her too hard about it. But at some point, he had a right to know about his father -- no matter how painful that discussion might be.

And how did the Hoodlum game tie into all of this? Someone obviously wanted him to find out about his mother's past, but who? Another wave of realization washed over him. Could the Gamemaster be his mysterious father? Maybe this was how he planned to reveal himself to Eddie. But why go through all of this Hoodlum nonsense? If the guy could arrange the laptop drop off and the money and pickup bag exchanges, he certainly had plenty of opportunities to communicate directly with Eddie.

It still made no sense, but Eddie promised himself to ask his mother some detailed questions about their past. He wouldn't let on that he knew about the Dolly, but he wanted to make it clear that he was old enough to know a few things and had a *right* to know them.

"Still with us, Mr. Ponzino? Charged particles moving through electromagnetic fields not electrifying enough to hold your attention?"

The question from his Physics teacher startled him, and he could feel his face flush.

"Yes, Mr. Nicholson. Sorry." Eddie heard scattered laughter at his expense. He still felt tired, but the embarrassing moment was enough to sharpen his attention for the rest of the class. The short walk down the hall to his next class, advanced U.S. History, took less than a minute. Before the class had even started, he had settled into a dreamlike state once again.

On top of the revelation from the Hello Dolly break-in, Eddie was still reeling from the terrible news Mike had told him on the way to school. Apparently, Mike's father was having an affair, and right now it looked like his parents were very likely headed towards a divorce. He could tell Mike was devastated. When Mike shared that the affair had been revealed during his father's presentation at the golf club, Eddie's heart had stopped. Was this all his fault? The USB drive he plugged into Andrew's computer almost certainly caused the whole mess. Jesus! And when Mike mentioned Jennifer Blackmoore's name, that clinched it. He didn't know exactly how it all tied together, but it had to be more than coincidence that the very next task had been at the Blackmoore's home. What the hell was going on? He had tried to say something supportive to Mike, but his words just felt knee-jerk and worthless.

If his father was the Gamemaster, why would he mess so badly with these other peoples' lives? Revealing his mother's dark past may have made sense, but why would he expose Mike's father's affair and wreck his golf course? And why did he try to frame some random high school kid for the crime? God only knows what the USB drive did to the Blackmoore's computer. He supposed that fun story had yet to break. He prayed that Mike and his family would never learn of his role in sabotaging Andrew's presentation. If offered the option, he would gladly confess to all of the other crimes if that one act could remain a secret forever.

If it weren't for Hoodlum and the far-reaching ugliness that the game had caused, he would have spent this day fondly remembering every moment of his Saturday with Emma and their first big kiss. Instead, all he felt was sympathy, shame, and guilt. He tried to tell himself that he really had no choice, and that he had pressed on with the game to protect Mike as much as himself. The justification felt false and shallow.

Seeing Emma in English class the following period restored his spirits significantly. And the playful little nudges and secret winks they exchanged during lunch reminded him of just how fantastic their date on Saturday had gone. They gazed at each other across their lunch table, boyfriend and girlfriend for all to see. Eddie sensed a little quiet hostility from the robot-like boy. Perhaps he had thought of Emma as his own. Emma didn't seem to notice, though, and greeted everyone at their table with her usual cheeriness before turning her attention back to Eddie.

"Did I tell you I figured out how we could do it?" Emma asked.

"How we could do what?" Eddie asked back, winking suggestively. He couldn't believe how brash he had gotten over the past few weeks. Pre-Hoodlum Eddie would never have dared to utter such a bold inference.

Emma punched his arm. "Not that, Mr. Perv! The picnic! To get your mom and Eric together?"

"Oh, right. What did you come up with?"

"Well, it would involve having more of a lunchtime or early afternoon picnic," she explained. "We could do it across the second shift break, and split the crowd into two different groups. We'd need to do a little more work, but that way Eric could be there for at least half of the picnic. And if we got him for the second half, maybe he would stay late with us and your mom, and help clean up!"

Emma was clearly excited about her plan, and looked at Eddie for his approval.

"That's perfect! Do you think your parents would like to come, too?"

"I'm sure they'd love to. Now we need to start planning the food!"

Eddie watched as Emma pulled a notebook from her bag and started making a detailed list of the picnic preparations. She asked him for his opinion on a detail or two, but otherwise scribbled furiously in her notebook for the rest of their lunch period. Again, it struck him how much she reminded him of his mother.

On the way back to their lockers, he asked her if she'd like to go to the lake on Saturday, then out for dinner somewhere. He had already given his shift to Steve again, so both he and Emma could have all day Saturday off. She not only agreed, but decided they would both meet each other's parents, too. He couldn't shake the feeling that any time he spent with Emma seemed like an incredible dream. Just being with her made his Hoodlum troubles seem trivial.

When he left her for his afternoon classes, he caught sight of Cindy in the hallway and instantly felt terrible again. Her eyes looked red and puffy, making him feel even shittier about his dreamlike times with Emma.

---

Once back home from school, Eddie wasted no time picking up the reward money for the strip club break in. The thick stack of hundred-dollar bills looked ridiculous, just tossed casually into a tattered bag alongside the Hoodlum PC. With over five thousand dollars now sitting in the dusty cabinet in his garage, he decided that he would need to address the cash storage situation today. No more procrastinating.

His concern about the next (and hopefully final) task had him completely on edge, so he figured that having a little distraction to work on while he waited for the details might help him relax.

He went inside to make dinner and check for solutions on the internet. He slid a pair of frozen pot pies in the oven and put together a halfway decent tossed salad. After a little careful internet browsing, he found the answer: a safe deposit box. He could get one at the same bank he and his mother used, and didn't need to open a new account. He'd never had one before, but he did watch Matt Damon use one in the "Bourne Identity." You could put whatever you wanted in it, and no one watched you put stuff in or take it out. He hoped there wasn't a minimum age requirement. It seemed like the perfect solution, at least until he figured out a clever way to explain the source of the money to his mother so they could just use it. He would see about getting one later this week.

His mother wouldn't be home for another fifteen minutes, so he went back to the garage to check the Hoodlum laptop again. Sure enough, the Gamemaster had acknowledged his reward pickup, and the next task was ready for him to view.

Eddie had dreaded this moment. He knew he would have to do whatever challenge the Gamemaster had planned, no matter how intimidating. When he advanced beyond the "next task" screen with the macabre symbols, the graphic display became a congratulatory salute, with virtual fireworks and a smiling skull wearing a party hat.

**CONGRATULATIONS, HOODLUM!**

**TASK #7 WILL BE YOUR FINAL CHALLENGE.
TASK REWARD: $5,000**

**AS PROMISED, ALL WILL BE REVEALED
WHEN THIS TASK HAS BEEN COMPLETED.**

**FOR TASK #7, YOU WILL ENTER THE
LAUFFERS' GARAGE AND "BORROW" THE LIMO
INSIDE. YOU WILL DRIVE THE LIMO TO THE GOLF
CLUB PARKING LOT AND LEAVE IT THERE.**

**TAKE NOTE: THE ONLY TIME TO COMPLETE
THIS TASK IS BETWEEN 5 AND 6PM THIS
WEDNESDAY, WHEN NO ONE WILL BE HOME AT
THE LAUFFER RESIDENCE.**

**AS BEFORE, YOU WILL NEED TO PICK UP A
PACKAGE OF SUPPLIES AND ADDITIONAL**

**INSTRUCTIONS AT THE USUAL SPOT. THIS CAN BE DONE ANY TIME BEFORE 5PM ON WEDNESDAY.**

**AS ALWAYS, GOOD LUCK, HOODLUM!**

**KIND REGARDS,**

*THE HOODLUM GAMEMASTER*

After the last two challenges, he expected much worse. This task could be done right here in Sutter Valley, and right next door. Compared to breaking into a cop's house or a strip club, this didn't seem too tough at all. Sure, if he got caught in the act he would get in trouble, but if the limo turned up in a neighborhood parking lot it could play out more like a prank than a real crime. This should be a piece of cake!

And getting another five thousand wouldn't hurt, either. For the first time in weeks, Eddie felt like he might finally be done with the whole Hoodlum mess, and even walk away with a very respectable supply of cash.

As his mother's car turned onto their street, he stashed the laptop back in the cupboard and headed in for dinner.

---

Monday nights at Silver's Grocery were typically slow, and tonight was no exception. While Steve manned the only open register, Eric had Eddie clean the glass windows on the deli cases and frozen food doors.

As planned, Eddie had ridden the moped to Silver's tonight so Steve could take it back home. Eddie hoped to hitch a ride back to his own house from anyone else that was closing tonight.

Glass cleaning bored Eddie, but it was easy. He wanted to talk to Steve during break. They grabbed bags of chips and headed back to the break room.

"Hey, Eddie. Haven't seen you much lately," Steve said. "Looks like you and Emma are a thing now, eh?"

"Yeah, Steve. Sorry I kind of dipped on you guys at lunch. I just started hanging out with her and…"

"Dude, don't worry," Steve interrupted. "Any one of us would have done the same thing if we got the chance. Emma is awesome. We're all just jealous." Steve offered up his fist for the bump.

"Thanks! It's definitely a new experience for me." Eddie proudly returned the bump. "I never woulda had the nerve if she wasn't so easy to talk to."

"I know what you mean. But you did it. And thanks to you, I'm gonna ask Jenny Griffin out. Maybe tomorrow. And Brian is going to ask out Heather McMillan, too. Who knows? By this time next week, our famous old table of nerds may be completely empty. All because of you."

Eddie knew Steve was half kidding, but it lifted his spirits to think that he was admired by his friends for his dating bravado. He took a deep bow to acknowledge his glory.

"Heather McMillan?" he asked. "I think she's a friend of Emma's from band. Does she play the trombone?"

"Maybe," Steve shrugged. "I think she goes to Brian's church, or something."

"Well Jenny's awesome, too. She kicked both our asses last year at the science fair with that robotic arm project. And she's pretty hot, too!"

"I noticed that," Steve said with a grin. "In fact, that was a key factor in my selection process."

Eddie laughed. "Good luck, Bro. She'd be crazy not to go out with you. And thanks again for loaning me the moped."

He walked back to clean more glass doors feeling quite proud of himself. Not only had he acquired his own girlfriend, he had initiated an overdue wave of testosterone among his nerd brethren.

Could it be that playing the Hoodlum game had brought him out of his shell? He supposed it was possible, but he had to at least give some credit to the advice and encouragement he got from Mike.

Thinking about Mike reminded him again of the drama at the Ashlands' house. He wondered if Mike suspected that the Hoodlum game had played a critical role in unraveling his family. Or, more accurately, the Hoodlum game and one of his most trusted friends. As Eddie's late grandfather used to say, that thought made him feel "lower than whale shit."

---

On Tuesday, Eddie didn't have to work. After school he jogged down to the fishing spot to pick up the last package. Dark clouds filled the sky, but so far it hadn't started to rain. He took a nostalgic look around, hoping that any future trips down here would only involve fishing, or maybe just sneaking a beer or two. Would Mike even be around to join him? He knew Emma would love it here.

He snatched the envelope and started back up the trail. The envelope contained the expected contents -- a security key, a set of car keys with a Lexus key chain, a detailed map of the Lauffers' property with the security system layout and a paragraph of instructions. The first heavy drops of rain began to fall, so he decided to wait 'til he got back to the garage to read them.

The instructions confirmed that the theft must occur Wednesday night between five and six o'clock. They included a code to disarm the alarm system. There was the usual "Good Luck, Hoodlum" garbage, and then one final paragraph.

**TAKE NOTE, HOODLUM. FOR THIS FINAL TASK, YOU ARE NOT TO WEAR A MASK OF ANY KIND. DOING SO WILL FORFEIT THE FINAL CHALLENGE AND PREVENT YOU FROM WINNING THE GAME. YOU ARE SO CLOSE, HOODLUM. DO NOT LOSE FAITH NOW!**

That last paragraph seemed very suspicious. If this was the final challenge, why did the Gamemaster care if he wore a mask or not? Was this really some television schtick after all? God dammit, he was so tired of trying to outguess the Gamemaster!

He thought about it and decided he wasn't too worried about the mask issue. He assured himself this big "theft" would ultimately be ruled as a relatively harmless prank… as long as he didn't get caught in the act, anyway. And even if he *was* recorded, he reasoned that this video would be less incriminating than others the Gamemaster already possessed. Or was it?

What if the Gamemaster or someone else stole the limo from the golf course parking lot? That would make Eddie an accessory to a very serious crime. Could that be the reason for the strange new rule, to frame him for the theft of a pricey Lexus? Maybe this last crime was the motivation for the whole game!

As always, he realized he had no choice in the matter. He would have to go through with it. Eddie reflected on the other tasks and all the information the Gamemaster had provided. When he thought it through, it didn't seem likely this could all be a frame-up job to steal a car. If the Gamemaster had this much info on everyone's security system, knowledge of when people would be away and even car keys to boot, he could probably take all the cars he wanted with very little risk.

Though these thoughts calmed him somewhat, he did want to prepare for his final confrontation with the Gamemaster. For that, he should try to get more info from his mother about his past. He couldn't quite accept that the Gamemaster might be his father, but he wanted to be prepared.

When he considered other possible reasons for the no-mask rule, he wondered if he would be greeted by the Gamemaster and a camera crew when he showed up at the golf course parking lot with the limo. They probably just wanted to see his facial reaction for the "big reveal." He had no idea how it would actually play out, but that seemed like the most likely scenario.

Eddie stashed the envelope and went inside to prepare the traditional Tuesday tacos. He decided to tell his mother that she could meet Emma on Saturday. He hoped that this news might encourage her to be more open about her past, whatever it might be.

---

"Hola, Amigo! Looks like you're already rolling on the tacos!" His mother hugged him before even setting her purse down.

"Buenos Dias, Madre. Have a good day?"

"It was OK. How 'bout you? Not working tonight, right?"

"Very good. And yes, not working tonight. Going on another date with Emma on Saturday, though. And bringing her by to meet you."

Tina's face lit up as though she had just won the lottery.

"That's the best news I've heard all day. I can't wait to meet her!"

"She's excited to meet you, too. And I know you'll love her. I'm gonna meet her parents too, then we're going to the lake. If I can borrow the car."

"Yeah, Baby, no problem! I'm so damn excited. And it's taco night!' She set her purse down and gave Eddie another huge hug.

He loved seeing her this happy. Despite his big plans for information gathering, he didn't have the heart to ask her a single thing about her mysterious past.

Whatever tomorrow had in store for him, he would just deal with it as it happened. Game on.

## Chapter 12 - Task Seven: Final Task?

Rather than cut straight across the lawns, Eddie chose to walk all the way down his own driveway and up the full length of the Lauffers'. The Gamemaster had promised an empty house at precisely 5pm. Eddie had no reason to doubt this; *almost* everything had played out exactly as the Gamemaster promised. Still, he wanted a reasonable cover story in case the Old Lady or one of her workers unexpectedly appeared -- especially since he couldn't wear a mask for this one. He had taken the time to find an old clipboard and even printed out a bogus petition for her to sign. Something about migratory bird sanctuary areas that he'd grabbed off the internet.

He followed the flagstone sidewalk from the driveway and climbed the stairs to the Lauffers' imposing front porch. The landscaping looked beautiful, yet somehow too perfect. He glanced across the porch to his own yard where random patches of clover and crabgrass dominated various sections of the lawn.

The Ponzino landscaping consisted of four scruffy bushes that reminded him of Charlie Brown's Christmas tree. No risk of offending nature with artificial perfection over there!

As he rang the doorbell it occurred to him that he had never even spoken to Old Lady Lauffer directly, despite living next door for so long. They had exchanged a few distant waves over the years, but she always hurried inside to avoid any possibility of conversation. The closest he had ever come was the strange encounter last week while mowing. He wondered what she must think of him and his mother.

Peering through the window along the side of the front entrance, he could see only darkness. No movement of any kind; no reaction to the doorbell. He paused a few seconds longer, then checked to see if any neighbors had noticed him. Again, no activity. He stepped off the porch and snuck down the sidewalk between the house and garage. The covered walkway led back to the gardens and to the rear entrance of the garage. He stopped again to listen and watch for any signs of life at all. Utter silence. The gardens still looked so different and open to him without the mermaid.

Now hidden from the street, he took his time. Sure enough, she too had an alarm system from O.L. Security. Not too "secure" for a security company. The Gamemaster seemed to know every code in the neighborhood. He wondered if that was a clue. The code worked as always. He found the garage back door key and put it in the lock when a thought struck him. If the Old Lady was out of the house, wouldn't her limo be gone, too? He tried to peek through the garage door window to check but saw only his own reflection. The Gamemaster had never been wrong, yet how else would she travel anywhere? Maybe someone picked her up? Now he wished he had watched out the window earlier. Whatever. Might as well quit worrying and get on with it.

He pushed the door and stepped inside. He intended to leave the door open; to allow himself enough light until he found a switch. Cold darkness filled the garage like a tomb. He took another step inside.

As he entered, the door slammed closed behind him with an audible click of the latch. What the hell? A quick check confirmed his worst fear -- the door had locked closed, with the key stupidly left in the outside lock. He was trapped like a fish in a barrel!

Would he have to wait here until the Old Lady or one of her workers opened the door? He could feel his face flush. Part of him worried that he'd be caught trespassing, possibly stealing. Another part of him worried about the game itself. He had come so close -- could it really end with him looking like a complete jackass? Would he have to face yet *another* challenge? He just couldn't accept that. Could he open the main door and get out?

He groped along the wall for a light switch but found nothing. Shit! Not even a helpful glow from a garage door opener? Trying not to panic, he took a tentative step towards the center of the garage. He still had the car keys. If he could find the limo, then the car door, he'd soon have all the light he needed. He reached out with his hands, expecting to feel cold metal. Nothing.

He took another careful step. Still nothing. Jesus, how big could this damn garage be? He started to worry that the Gamemaster might be wrong, for once. As he lifted his foot to take another step, bright light from everywhere blinded him.

"Hello, Edward!"

Eddie almost screamed. The intensely lit garage stood completely empty, except for two chairs in the middle and a small briefcase between them. In one of the chairs sat Old Lady Lauffer herself, holding a laptop computer and grinning with obvious pleasure.

"Mrs. Lauffer! Hi! I uh, have a petition…" he stammered. He fumbled with the clipboard, regretting he hadn't taken time to learn the details of his bogus cover story. He could feel his heart pounding in his chest. How could he possibly explain breaking into her garage for a petition signature?

"Never mind that horseshit, my boy. I'm the Hoodlum Gamemaster, and I know exactly why you're here. I brought you here! Now take a seat so we can chat." She patted her hand on the vacant chair.

Eddie felt like she had just slugged him in the gut. He considered making a run for it, but then remembered the locked door. And what would be the point? If the Old Lady truly was the Gamemaster, she held all the cards anyway. He settled into the seat, still in shock.

"Bet you didn't think it was me, did you?" she cackled.

"No. Not in a million years. We didn't think you knew how to program computers. And you had us steal your own statue, and then your limo!"

The old woman laughed again. "The Mermaid? I hated that gaudy tramp. One of my late husband's only contributions to the gardens. I'm glad to be rid of it, and I hoped it would convince you that I wasn't behind all of this. I even called the sheriff to make it look good. Did it work?"

"It sure did, Mrs. Lauffer. We had ruled you out pretty early on."

"Oh, we're going to be much closer now, you and me. Please call me Olivia. And it was my own son that got me into programming many years ago. So much has changed since then, but I've had plenty of time to learn." She pressed a few keys on the laptop, and the extreme brightness dimmed to a much more pleasant level. A multicolored array of lights began to pulse in a rhythmic pattern around the perimeter of the garage ceiling. Classical music played through speakers from somewhere up above.

"So, you were able to program the Hoodlum laptop so that it could erase itself if we broke the rules, and all that stuff?" Eddie still couldn't quite accept the revelation, and Olivia seemed to enjoy explaining her elaborate plan. Her computer driven light show impressed him, too. He wondered what other little surprises she had planned.

"Oh, I suppose I could have figured that out, but I just bluffed that part. The stuff I did for the Hoodlum game could be easily done by any hacker worth her salt."

"You always seemed to be one step ahead of us. Like when I planted the camera to catch you at the payoff pickup on the fourth hole tee."

Olivia leaned back in her chair, clapped her hands and laughed again. "It never occurred to you boys that I could listen to every word you said when you were near the computer, did it?" She wiped her eyes and continued. "Your little camera scheme was easy to avoid, thanks to you telling me all about it."

He did feel foolish for not thinking of that. And both he and Mike thought the name "Hoodlum" seemed like something an older person would say. Jesus! He still couldn't believe Old Lady Laufer was the goddam *Gamemaster*.

"But why?" Eddie asked. "It doesn't make any sense. Why did you have us tear up the golf course, and frame Geoff St. Vincent for it?"

"Well, I've never been a big fan of that damn golf course. And as for framing Geoff? That one, my dear, I did for you."

"For me?"

"Edward, it's no secret that you've been pining for that young Ashland girl for months now. And I don't blame you – she is a cute little thing. I heard you talk about the St. Vincent boy's plans for her, and I wanted to take that oafish brute out of the picture for you. Of course, I had also hoped that by doing all these tasks, you'd get up the stones to ask the girl out on your own by now." She shot him a disapproving look.

Eddie blushed, embarrassed that he had been so transparent about Cindy, and by the fact that Olivia thought of him as cowardly. She knew so much, yet she didn't seem to know that he did, in fact, have a girlfriend. He decided not to bring it up now.

"How do you know all this stuff? I never see you leave your house!"

"Oh, I have eyes and ears in more places than your little Hoodlum computer. Guess who owns the contract security service for the Sutter Valley Golf Club? And the Hello Dolly?" She smiled and cocked her head playfully. O.L. Security is my own company. She pressed more keys on the laptop, and showed him the screen. The display showed a dashboard of security camera views from dozens of locations throughout the neighborhood. That seemed a bit creepy!

"The O.L. is for Olivia Lauffer?" he asked.

"You're lookin' at her!"

Her smirking blue eyes seemed intense and youthful. Eddie imagined that she had been quite an attractive lady in her day. Her widespread security influence certainly explained how she had access to everyone's codes. And God knows what else.

"More than anything, Edward, I wanted this game to build your self-confidence. You already know you're a very bright young man, but I wanted to show you just how strong and capable you can be. You have so much potential, Edward."

"But why us? You must have picked us on purpose for your game. You left the laptop bag right where we fish."

"Well of course I picked you. And I'll tell you why in just a few minutes." Olivia checked her watch.

"What happens in a few minutes?"

"Someone else will be joining us. Any minute now. Edward, would you mind pulling over that third chair?"

Eddie stood to get the chair. He wondered who it could be. He hoped it wasn't Mike; he really didn't want to have to reveal his part in exposing his father's affair. But who else could it be? Cindy? That would be even more humiliating. A cop? That didn't make sense, either. After learning that Old Lady Lauffer was the Gamemaster, almost nothing would surprise him now. Before he had much time to guess, the overhead garage door opener roared to life.

He had to wait a few seconds for the rising door to fully reveal the mystery guest. He could see a woman in familiar-looking slacks, then her purse and the garage door remote she held in her hand. Finally, ...the face. His mother! Was she in on this, too? Her expression changed from confused to furious when she recognized Eddie inside.

"Eddie! What are you doing over here?" Her head snapped to Olivia. "I thought we had a deal, you old witch!"

"Settle down, Tina. There has been a new development." Olivia waved for her and Eddie to take their seats. "I haven't told Edward anything yet."

Tina sat down, but she still looked angrier than Eddie had ever seen her.

"Told me anything about what?" Eddie asked.

"We'll get to that. Let me catch your mother up on recent events."

While Tina glared, Olivia explained to her the nature of the Hoodlum game, and how she had manipulated Eddie and Mike to complete several challenging tasks around the neighborhood. Thankfully, her description made it sound as though these tasks were character-building exercises that benefited both the boys and the community at large. To his relief, she did not describe any vandalism, burglary, breaking and entering or other specific crimes he had committed. To his even greater relief, his mother did not ask.

Tina looked back at Olivia. "OK, so you exploited a little loophole in our 'no direct contact' agreement, but why is he here now? I'd call this pretty goddam close direct contact! What's this big 'new development'?"

Olivia folded her hands on her laptop. She looked at the floor for a long moment, then directly at Tina.

"I'm dying, Tina. I don't expect you'll be too concerned about that, but I have no family. My doctor says I've got less than a year left."

Olivia was not grinning or gloating now. Her eyes welled up and she looked from Tina to Eddie.

Tina barely showed any reaction. "I'm sorry to hear that, but how does that change anything? Thanks to you, I don't have the family that I should have, either." She stood and reached out to take Eddie's hand to leave.

Eddie had no intention of leaving. His mind rocked with the last few comments from both women. He had dozens of questions, and he refused to budge before hearing some detailed answers.

"Wait, Mom. I'm not going yet. What are you not telling me?"

Tina winced. "I hate you for this." She glared at Olivia, then sat back in the chair and stared at the floor with her arms folded.

"He has the right to know, Tina." Olivia said. "I invited you here, so you could tell your side, too. But he has every right to know."

"Jesus, a right to know what? Just tell me what's going on!" It all seemed surreal to Eddie. He could imagine them suddenly laughing at him, while some reality show tv crew stepped out from behind a fake wall in the garage. Everything just seemed that crazy.

"This is all about your father, Edward. My son, Karl." Olivia leaned back in her chair, giving Eddie time to process the information.

Tina sat with her hands clasped, watching Eddie. The possibility that this could be some television prank had just dropped to zero. This had to be genuine. Both women sat rock still, awaiting his reaction. Understanding slowly washed over him. For the first time in his life, he realized how people could actually faint from hearing shocking news. His head flooded with even more questions.

"So… you're my grandmother?" he finally asked.

"That's right, Edward." Olivia brightened, overjoyed to finally share their secret connection. "I'm your grandma."

Eddie turned back to Tina. "But my last name's Ponzino. Why isn't it Lauffer? How come you never told me about my father?"

"Ponzino is my maiden name, as you know." Tina sniffed and dabbed at her eyes. "I left that on the birth certificate when I brought you back here. That was part of the deal."

"Back from where? What deal?"

"Your mother believes I'm responsible for your father's death," explained Olivia. "She moved away to Georgia when she was pregnant with you, to live with her father, and that's where you were born."

"To hide him from you and your husband!" Tina snapped. "You rich bastards think you can do anything you want, and break the law, and destroy peoples' lives, just so it all works out the way you want it to. That's bullshit!"

"We had lost our only son," Olivia said. Eddie could tell she struggled to keep from shouting back herself. "We couldn't stand the thought of losing our grandson, too."

"So they tracked me down like a criminal," Tina continued. "And they promised me. *Promised* me!" She pointed an angry finger at Olivia. "You promised you would never talk to him or tell him about your relationship as long as I agreed to live next door." She turned to Eddie. "I didn't have a job, or any way to even get one when you were a baby. I needed the cash, so I agreed. I hated myself for it, after what they did to your father, but I really had no choice."

"That's why you guys always just waved and went inside whenever I came out in the yard," Eddie reflected. He tried to remember what her husband looked like, but it was just too long ago.

Olivia nodded. "Your grandfather wanted so much to take you fishing, to ball games, picnics, all the fun things that grandpas do. To have you so close and not be able to even speak to you might have been harder on him than just not knowing you at all. I am so sorry both of you missed out on that."

"Eddie *did* have a grandfather that did all of those things with him," Tina said. "He never got to do any of those things with his daddy, though!" She started crying, and Eddie put his hand on her shoulder.

He could feel his own voice tremble, but he still had so many questions.

"Mom, you did a great job raising me by yourself. I never needed anyone but you."

Tina turned and hugged him but continued crying. Eddie teared up too, but he looked over her shoulder to Olivia.

"So, what happened to my father?"

Olivia reached into the bag on the floor and produced a framed photograph of a young man. The man stood a little shorter than average height, with a slender build. He had Eddie's messy hair and the same brown eyes. He wore jeans and an untucked tee shirt with a Grateful Dead emblem. To Eddie, he looked a little nerdier than he'd always imagined, but he could see a resemblance. He held the picture for several moments, mesmerized. As recently as this morning, he had never expected to know anything about his father, much less hold a picture of him in his hands.

"Your father was a brilliant computer programmer," Olivia explained. "Way ahead of his time. And back then they didn't have classes for it like they do now. He had to teach himself. My husband knew the electrical business backwards and forwards, and he had made a fortune at it. But he never had anywhere near your father's ability. We knew Karl was destined for greatness, and I suppose that's why we were so determined to pick out just the right girl for him."

"What she's *not* saying is that they knew I was the *wrong* girl," Tina sneered. "Didn't have enough money, or a Harvard degree, or a family pedigree going back to the Pilgrims."

"Oh, it was a little more than that, Tina. And Edward knows, too. One of his tasks was to do a little family history research, right Eddie?"

Tina turned to Eddie. "What is she talking about? What family history do we have?"

"I'm talking specifically about employment history," Olivia said.

Tina closed her eyes. "Eddie…" she stammered.

Eddie finally realized what Olivia referred to. The records at the strip club!

"It's OK, Mom. I found out about the job at the dance club. Don't feel bad about it."

Tina dropped her head in her hands while Olivia continued.

"I told your mother she'd get the chance to tell her side, and I'm asking you both to let me tell my own. And part of my story is that your mother didn't just work at the club, she was one of the headline dancers. So, no, we didn't need our son to marry a girl with family ties back to the Pilgrims, but we did *not* want him to settle down with a stripper!"

"But Karl loved me, and we were so happy. You both knew that!" Tina shouted.

"It's possible that he did, and I'm sorry, but we believed he deserved better."

Eddie again put his hand on his mother's shoulder, and she clasped it with her own. As painful as he knew this must be for her, he really needed to hear the whole story.

"When your father was about your age, he hadn't even met your mother," Olivia continued. "My husband and I were very close friends with the Sutter family. You might recall that they were the ones responsible for designing the golf course and clubhouse. Very well thought of by the whole community, though there were only about a dozen houses around here back then. The Sutters had a lovely daughter about Karl's age named Jennifer. To your mother's point, she did come from very good stock, she was beautiful by all accounts, and had the brains and the drive to go to a fine college," Olivia explained.

"Sounds like the perfect match," Tina said with more than a little sarcasm.

"That's what we thought," Olivia continued. "And her parents did, too. But young Jennifer had plans of her own. When Karl tried to talk to her, she dismissed him rather rudely, saying outright that she had no interest in him at all. She had devastated him, and shortly after that he began visiting your mother's dance club."

"We didn't meet at the club. You make it sound like I was a hooker!" Tina sat up straight in the chair, determined to give her own account. "We met when he stopped to help me when my piece of crap car broke down in the rain. I had just moved out here on my own. My mother had died years before, and I just got tired of fighting with my father all the time. I came here because a friend had promised me a decent job at the canning factory. The place went out of business less than a month later, so I started out at the 'Hello Dolly' club as a waitress. The manager of the club told me I could make five times as much if I was willing to dance, so I did it. Maybe I should've felt worse about it, but when you're eighteen and making minimum wage with no other job options, the choice seemed pretty obvious to me. And even if I hadn't run away from home, there was no 'fine college' in my future, like that Jennifer girl had." Tina seemed to find new strength as she described the tough circumstances of her own past.

Eddie hoped that she knew how proud he was of her, and how much he loved her.

"Well, I certainly had no admiration for Jennifer Sutter after she broke my Karl's heart," Olivia added. "And I knew eventually she would reveal herself as the self-centered little tramp that I knew her to be. Edward helped see to that, didn't you?"

"What is she talking about?" Tina asked.

Eddie's mind raced. The only task that could have possibly revealed someone as a tramp was... Mike's father's affair! But that woman's name was Blackmoore, the wife of Hot Rod Blackmoore. Sutter must have been her maiden name!

"You mean Jennifer Blackmoore?" he asked Olivia.

"The very same. And as much as I enjoyed exposing that little hussy, I really do feel bad about the pain it may have caused your friend Mike, and his family. I hope that they can get through this."

Eddie hoped so, too. He worried that a divorce could mean his fiend Mike would move away forever. He wanted to hate Olivia for that, but he knew he shared part of the blame himself.

Tina still looked confused. She shrugged and shook her head, waiting for more explanation.

"One of the tasks in the Hoodlum game was to plant the video of Mike's father and Jennifer in his presentation at the club," Olivia explained. "That's how everyone found out about their affair."

"I swear I didn't know that's what it was!" Eddie pleaded. "It was supposed to be fake information about the golf course vandalism. Just a prank! I didn't realize 'til later what it really was, or I never would have done it."

"Yes, to be fair, Edward just played the role of delivery boy on that one. I took advantage of the fact that he had easy access to the Ashlands' home."

Eddie cringed at that, feeling more guilty than ever that he had betrayed his friend's trust. The disappointed look on his mother's face told him she felt the same way.

"Well, back to the night when I first met your father," Tina continued. "He stood out in the pouring rain and tried to get my car started, but it was shot. I couldn't believe how sweetly he treated me, compared to most of the pushy jerks I met at the club. He took me to the diner to get a late supper and drove me home. He felt bad dropping me off at my dark little trailer. I could tell he was worried for me, but he didn't try to talk his way inside like a lot of guys would. I told him I was very safe and used to it. He gave me his number to call if I ever needed help again."

"So you called him back?" Eddie asked.

"I didn't have to. By the time I got home from work the next night, he had fixed my car up and left it in front of my trailer with a bouquet of flowers on the front seat. Even filled up the tank with gas. Nobody had ever done anything like that for me before, and I was really touched. After that, we would meet and go for walks and dinners and things. I thought I was keeping my job at the Dolly secret from him. I felt embarrassed about it when I was around him. Somehow, he found out though. Or somebody told him. Probably you." She looked at Olivia.

"No, all of this was before his father and I realized what was going on."

"Well, however he found out, he was OK with it. I thought that would be the last I ever saw him, but he stayed with me and told me it didn't matter. He never let on that he was rich, but I could tell he wanted to take me away from that old trailer park and my job at the club. He didn't ask me to marry him, like a formal proposal, but he asked casually if I would ever consider something like that. I told him I would, but I wanted to know more about him, too. I wanted to meet his folks." Tina sniffed and shook her head with regret.

"And that's when we got involved," Olivia jumped in. "We found out about Tina and what she did for a living. We were mortified! I know it sounds cruel, but we had to think about our family name and the reputation of the business that my husband had worked so hard to build."

"So you turned against your own son, and whatever happiness he may have had," Tina jabbed.

"I realize how terrible this sounds now, but at the time we really believed this was an impetuous romance, brought on by Jennifer Sutter's heartless rejection. We didn't honestly believe he was in love with your mother. So, we had a plan."

"You see, Eddie? Rich people always need to control everything and everyone. Consequences don't matter, only intentions. And it's always 'for the best,' right?"

Eddie hoped that the women would continue with the story. He worried that one of them, most likely his mother, would provoke the other one enough to erode the discussion into a screaming match. If that happened, he might never learn the answers that he still needed to hear.

"I admit that we acted rashly, and I've regretted our decision every day of my life. I'm sure you know that, Tina. And up until now, we have honored your conditions because of what happened."

"What happened?" Eddie asked. "What was the plan?"

Olivia hesitated for a moment, collecting herself. "We wanted to convince Karl that your mother was a con artist, using him to dig her way into the family fortune. We hired a local man to act as a private investigator. He had drummed up evidence…"

"*Fake* evidence!" Tina interjected.

"We left that to him. We arranged for him to confront Karl with the evidence, but Karl refused to hear any of it." Now Olivia looked as though she was going to break down. "You must understand," she continued. "We were so desperate."

"They had him bash the door into my place when Karl was staying over," Tina interrupted. "In the middle of the night, for God's sake! This big guy pulls a gun on Karl, and says he has proof that I'm running some kind of scam on him, and Karl damn well better listen to what he has to say."

"The gun and brutality were never part of our plan," Olivia said, her voice breaking.

"Well, he was there on your dime, so you own it. Everyone was yelling. I told Karl that it wasn't true, and your hired thug smashed my face with the butt of the gun. Karl grabbed for the gun to protect me, and the guy shot him point blank in the chest. He died in my arms on the floor of that two-bit trailer home, and the people responsible for it just walked away. And that was it." Tina openly sobbed, and Eddie hugged her.

"I know that's how you see it, Tina, and I can never change your mind."

"Because that's how it happened! Your little plan to break us up backfired, and your son is dead because of you! Now, you don't have a son, I don't have a husband, and Eddie never even got to *meet* his father!"

"As I've said, I have regretted what we did every day since, and my husband did, too. Even though we never told our hired man to break into your trailer, or to pull a gun, ultimately the responsibility rests with us. But you've made us pay for it, Tina. Do you know what it's been like to watch our only grandchild from a distance? To never talk to him, to never share his birthdays, to never even let him know we exist? I can assure you that we've suffered painfully for the part we played."

Eddie still had so many questions. "How could the guy that shot him just walk away?"

"Oh, that's the best part, Eddie." Tina pulled away from Eddie's hug to face Olivia. "Turns out their hired man was a cop. He made it very clear to me that I would take the fall for this unless I packed up and got the hell out of town. He called your husband and told him what happened, and that it was *my* fault. So your husband and he decided that would be the cleanest way to cover it up. Then I told him just what I told Karl earlier that night. That I was pregnant. The cop didn't even care. Told me to pack up and get out, or I would go to jail for murder. And who would believe my story? I was just some stripper that was trying to con my way into the Lauffer money, right? And I'm sure more money changed hands after that. The papers said that Karl had drowned in the lake. No autopsy, no trial, no investigation, that was it. Goodbye Karl. And good riddance to the floozie that he knocked up, too. We can't have any tacky loose ends when it comes to the Lauffer family reputation."

"You sent my mother away, pregnant with no money and no job?" asked Eddie.

"Edward, please try to imagine our state of mind," Olivia said. "Our only son had just been killed. We were utterly destroyed. After we came to terms with the shock of Karl's death, we realized that the only thing we had left of him was his child. We had your mother tracked down. A different man this time, of course, and it wasn't easy. She had moved back to her home town, but we didn't know where that was. It took nearly a year to find her, and by that time you'd been born. We made her a very generous offer. She could have lived here with us, and never worked another day in her life. But she wanted to punish us for

Karl, so we agreed to her 'no contact' deal. So, you came back to live next door, and we got her set up with a job nearby. A decent, respectable job."

"And nothing ever happened to the cop that shot my father?"

"Not until very recently. In fact, he went on to marry the same girl that shunned my Karl."

"Jennifer Sutter?" Once again, Eddie felt like he'd been slapped in the face. "Roddy Blackmoore was the cop that killed him?" He collapsed in his seat. "Didn't he say anything when my mother moved back here?"

"Oh, he knew well enough to keep quiet. Remember, he had already passed off Karl's death as a drowning. He didn't know the details of our little arrangement, but he understood that he was to leave your mother alone."

"So, you got a two-for-one deal," Tina said. "You got back at both Jenny *and* Roddy by showing the video of the affair. You're really good at wrecking peoples' lives, aren't you?" Tina seemed to find some humor in that.

"Well, with Edward's help, I did a little more than that."

This time, Eddie already knew what was coming. "What was on that thumb drive?"

Olivia smiled. "A treasure trove of illegal bookmaking, child pornography, black market deals, you name it. And I made sure to send an active ping to the link at the FBI scan center, so they'll be paying ol' Roddy a visit very soon. If they haven't already."

Eddie sensed that Tina brightened at that news, but he felt overwhelmed by it all.

He couldn't reconcile the friendly cop that came into their kindergarten classroom, the guy that had driven him home when he crashed his bike when he was nine, the Little League and soccer coach, the man he had always pictured as the face of honesty and justice; that *this* guy had killed his father and smashed his pregnant mother in the face with a pistol. His other little challenge had already thrown their family into turmoil with the Ashland affair business, and now this. He understood Olivia and Tina's hatred for the man, but for Eddie that was a lifetime ago. Now the Blackmoore kids would suffer the consequences, and never even know why. And Eddie himself had contributed to getting their father in serious trouble with the law and revealing their mother's affair.

On the other hand, Roddy had gotten away with killing his father and covering it up, and he had never answered for the crime. He should have paid a high price for that. Both his mother and Olivia felt that retribution was long overdue. And Eddie hadn't done anything to cause Jennifer and Mike's father's extramarital affair; he had simply helped to make it known publicly. But their kids hadn't had anything to do with either of these crimes, yet they were sure to pay for them in ways he could not even imagine. Would Roddy be sent to prison? Would the family lose their house? Their parents would almost certainly divorce. The Ashlands could be in a similar situation, also thanks to Eddie's greed for Hoodlum reward money.

While completing the first few tasks, Eddie had felt a sense of pride and accomplishment that seemed just as rewarding to him as the cash. He had rationalized those first few challenges as victimless, or relatively harmless. Now he began to hate himself for what he had become; a selfish kid who cared only about getting cash – even if it meant hurting people.

"Do you think he'll go to jail?" he asked Olivia.

"I sure hope so. I'm sure he'll fight it and try to blame someone else. And he's probably already lawyering up for his wife's affair."

"For once, I agree with her," added Tina. "I know you think he's a good guy now, Eddie, but I promise you he isn't. After he shot Karl and was talking to Karl's father about how to handle the whole mess, I heard him whisper that he could take care of me, too. Might've made things even easier for their little cover up. I don't know if your husband talked him out of it just because of the baby, or if he just didn't want his son's body discovered in the trailer home of a stripper. Either way, Roddy is a heartless prick who deserves to rot in jail."

"What about Tom and Karen?" Eddie asked.

Olivia's eyes squinched and she leaned forward in her chair. To Eddie it looked as though she worried that she had overlooked an important detail.

"Who?" she asked.

"Roddy and Jennifer's kids. Tom is a senior with a baseball scholarship, and Karen is a freshman. What will happen to them, now that their mom was caught cheating on her husband, and their dad is probably going to jail. What about them?"

Olivia seemed to relax, relieved that this was just Eddie's guilty conscience and not some flaw in her planning.

"Well, I suppose Rodney and Jennifer should have thought about that before they started sleeping around and shooting people. Their kids are not my problem. I just want justice for my son. Don't you want that, after what he did to both of your parents?"

"I dunno," Eddie answered. Tina gave his hand a supportive squeeze.

"See, that's how the rich folks do it, Eddie," she said. "Do whatever the hell you want and let the chips fall where they may. If there's any real trouble, just spend some cash to bribe or buy your way out of it. No harm done, right?"

Olivia waved a hand dismissively. "Well, the world is tough on all of us. Everything that I planned was to make people pay for the wrongs they've done; mostly to my son."

"You don't need to tell my son that the world is a tough place!" Tina barked. "We've both had it pretty tough, thanks to you. And now you want us to feel sorry for you, now that you're dying. Well maybe that's what the tough world had in store for you, since you decided to play God with so many other peoples' lives."

Olivia didn't have an argument for that. She looked defeated, and for the first time that Eddie had noticed, old and weak. Eddie agreed with his mother, to an extent. Olivia's manipulations had been entirely self-serving, even if somewhat justified. But she now represented the only other living person in his small family. He felt sorry for her, knowing that she didn't have long to live, but also for himself. After all, he had only just met his grandmother. Now, the "tough world" might soon take her away from him, too. He hoped that this conversation would not be their last. But the way things were going, he didn't think his mother would allow any further contact.

On top of that, he hadn't quite decided if he should be angry with his mother. She must have known how much it meant to him to learn about his past, but she had taken great measures to ensure that would never happen. Did her own hatred of the Lauffers warrant keeping him in the dark for so long? Did she really believe that they would have been a corrupting influence, or did she just want to punish them from killing the man she loved?

He didn't want her to think for even a moment that he was ashamed of her past, but she could no longer pretend that these shocking events had never happened. And if she hadn't insisted on her firm 'no direct contact' policy, Eddie could have enjoyed years of something like a real family life. And it had been so close to him all this time!

"So, what happens now?" he asked. "I'd still like to come over here and talk to Mrs. Lau – Olivia. Maybe she can even teach me some cool computer stuff."

Olivia smiled at him, then looked as though she was about to cry. Tina shook her head slowly, but Eddie could tell that she hadn't completely decided. It probably occurred to her that she really had no way of stopping Eddie, now that he knew the truth.

"Whatever you decide, I think you've earned this," Oliva said, reaching into the bag. She handed Eddie a manila envelope and the picture of Karl.

Eddy recognized the envelope as one of the payoff envelopes that she'd used for the Hoodlum rewards. He opened it and peeked inside. He pulled out a banded stack of one hundred-dollar bills.

"But I never completed the final task," he said. "I didn't earn this."

"Oh, you've more than earned it, Edward. And when I go, there'll be plenty more. After all, you are the sole heir to the family businesses. I sold them years ago, but I did quite well."

Until that moment, Eddie hadn't even considered the fact that his newly acquired grandmother would likely bequeath him a sizeable fortune. He would be rich! Once again, he felt a strong pang of guilt for thinking so greedily. He hoped that he could spend time talking to his grandmother, learning more about his father and grandfather. He wanted her to live a long time, even if she had proven herself uncaring of most other people. After all, it was obvious that she cared about him. Why else would she have gone to such great lengths to meet him face to face?

"I'll take the picture, but not the money," he finally said.

Both women looked at him with surprise.

"I didn't earn it, and I don't feel very good about the other money you gave me. I think I get why you did all this stuff, but I don't want to take any more money for all the trouble that I caused." He handed the envelope back to Olivia.

"And I really do want to learn more about my father, and maybe just talk to you sometimes."

Olivia took the envelope back. "I'd really like that, Edward. If it's OK with your mother."

"Well, I guess the 'no contact' deal is pretty much over anyway," Tina said. "It's fine with me if you want to visit. You just showed me that you're grown up enough to make your own choices." She stood and picked up her purse.

"Uh..." Eddie stammered, turning back to Olivia. "Is it OK if we still fish in your pond?"

"Of course, Edward." Olivia smiled and gave him a little aristocratic finger-wave goodbye.

Eddie put his arm around his mother's shoulder and they walked down the driveway in the fading sunlight.

# Chapter 13 - Loose Ends

Eddie spent most of Thursday morning in a daze. He had eaten dinner and watched TV with his mother after their explosive afternoon with Olivia, but neither of them had mentioned the Lauffers or the Hoodlum game at all. The whole affair had become the biggest "elephant in the room" scenario Eddie could imagine.

That seemed fine by him. At least for now. He needed some time to just let everything sink in. He supposed his mother needed a little time too. After all, she hadn't had much warning to prepare herself for the big confrontation. She did give him an extra-long hug before turning in, though, and reminded him about meeting Emma on Saturday.

Eddie sat through four classes before joining Emma for lunch, but couldn't remember a single detail from any of them. He could not stop thinking about his father. Did Karl Lauffer go to this school? Probably not. He didn't think Sutter Valley had its own school district back then. Maybe Karl had once considered the military, too. Or had he always planned to be a computer wizard? Eddie started to make a mental list of questions to ask Olivia the next time he saw her. It still freaked him out to think that he had a grandma!

He also wanted to talk to her about programming arial drones. He and Steve Kagasimi had been checking them out online, and he was intrigued. What could be cooler than a flying drone that you programmed to fly itself? Eddie thought that might be a great way to spend a little of his Hoodlum money. And he no longer had to worry about explaining the mysterious extra cash to his mother. He planned to put most of it into their regular account. She would probably be shocked to learn how much he had "earned" by playing the game.

While on the way from English to lunch, Emma told Eddie that she had convinced Eric to come to the picnic the following Saturday. He had agreed to switch off with the assistant manager so that everyone could go, and gave Emma huge credit for thinking up a way to include the entire staff without shutting down the store. It looked like the whole thing just might work out!

Now more than ever, Eddie wanted to get Eric and his mom together. Seeing how broken up his mother looked when she talked about Karl opened his eyes to how lonely she must feel. And for so long! Eddie believed that if he just put them close to one another for a little while, things would naturally take care of themselves. But for all his good intentions, he had never been able to make that moment happen. If Emma hadn't taken charge of the whole picnic operation, it never would have materialized. She would deserve all the credit if their matchmaking scheme worked out.

"My mother is so excited to meet you that she may actually explode before Saturday," he told Emma as they sat down.

"Aww. I can't wait to meet her, too. My mom literally couldn't wait to meet you. She stalked you at Silvers right after our first date. She said you seemed like a very sweet and caring young man." Emma reached out like an elderly relative and pinched his cheek. "I can tell my dad's a little nervous about it, but I just know you two will totally click."

"I'm sure we will." He reached over and squeezed Emma's hand.

Eddie wished he could share the exciting new developments in his life with Emma, but he didn't know how. There was simply no way to tell her just part of the story without including the embarrassing Hoodlum mess, and he wasn't ready to share that yet. He did feel more confident in their relationship with each passing day, but right now this seemed like too much. On top of his own criminal activities, he would have to reveal that his mother was a stripper, his neighbor turned out to be his dying grandmother, who not only participated in the accidental shooting death of his father, but was also a computer guru that had the whole community wired to monitor their secrets! Poor Emma would be forced to conclude that her new boyfriend was batshit crazy. What other explanation could there possibly be? He promised himself that he would tell her the whole story... someday. But not just yet.

After lunch, Emma gave him a quick kiss and told him she'd see him later at work. He could peripherally see other guys watching him get kissed. Not long ago, he would have been one of those guys, wondering if they would ever find an Emma of their own. He couldn't believe how much his world had changed in just a week or two. In so many ways.

He walked past his old table of fellow nerds to dump his trash. Only two of the former crew remained. Kevin and Ron were both Freshman, and appeared to be more interested in their phones than in any of the people around them.

Steve had called it; the others must have followed Eddie's example and left the safety of the nerd table to pursue the fairer sex. Sure enough, Steve himself sat only a few tables away, talking a mile a minute to the lovely Jenny Griffin. He happened to catch Eddie's eye as he passed and gave him a knowing wink. Eddie couldn't help but smile. Apparently, he wasn't the only one to push new limits.

---

Eddie and Tina enjoyed an early dinner, talking about meeting Emma on Saturday and hosting the picnic the following weekend. Having real topics to discuss made it easier to simply ignore everything that had taken place the day before.

"Are you sure you don't want me to help plan all of this?" Tina asked. "I feel like you and Emma are doing everything."

"It's all covered, Mom. Her parents have a bunch of tables and chairs, and Mike is letting us use their big grill. She loves doing this kind of thing, and I can use some of the Hoodlum money to cover the food. We just want you to relax and have a great time. You know most of the people already, and you'll get to meet Emma's parents."

Tina made her worried face.

"Have you met them yet? Do they seem nice?"

"I'll meet them on Saturday. I'm sure they're very nice. And Eric will be here, too. I think you guys would really like each other. He insisted on donating the burgers and dogs."

Tina tilted her head and squinted at Eddie.

"Is that what this is all about? Fixing your old lady up with your boss?" She leaned back in her chair, grinning at Eddie's discomfort.

"Mom, just like I said, I think you guys would really like each other. No pressure at all. Just give it a chance."

"Oh, you guys are so cute. Is Emma part of this, too? Eric does seem like a great guy. And he's one of your biggest fans. He always tells me how smart you are and how hard you work. I promise I'll talk to him."

"Cool, Mom. That's all I ask."

Eddie hadn't planned to spill the beans about his plans for them to meet, but his mother seemed receptive to the idea. Emma would be psyched.

"What time do you need to be at work, Eddie-bear?"

"Not 'til seven. I may go down to the pond for a few casts. Not many fishing days left."

"Knock 'em dead, Bud. I got the dishes."

"Thanks, Mom!"

---

Eddie had to move the seed bucket out of the way to get to his fishing gear inside the shed. Seeing the bucket reminded him to ask Olivia if he could use the Hoodlum laptop as a real computer. If not, getting a new desktop PC would be another great use of the Hoodlum cash. He grabbed his rod and tacklebox and backed out of the shed. When he closed the door, a tall figure appeared behind it.

"Jesus, Mike, you scared the shit out of me!"

"Sorry, Ghetti." Mike sounded sincere, but laughed a little too. "Looks like you're headed down to the pond. Mind if I join ya?"

"Absolutely, Bro. Come on down!"

It took Mike less than a minute to collect his gear and rejoin Eddie. Per tradition, he started to skirt around the far side of their yards to avoid being seen. He gave Eddie a puzzled look as he watched him boldly stride across his yard to the Lauffer's property.

"No need to worry," Eddie explained. "She knows we fish down there. She said we can go whenever we want."

"Really?" Mike asked. "That's cool." He followed Eddie behind the Lauffer's gardens and straight to the path in the woods.

They had exchanged hallway greetings over the past week or so, but Eddie hadn't had a genuine conversation with Mike since he told him about his father's affair. He hoped this would be a chance to clear the air between them, but he felt nervous, too. He had no idea where things stood between Mike's parents at this point. Everyone knew about the scandal. Eddie didn't want to bring it up, but he knew he had to say something.

"Mike, I don't know what to say about your mom and dad. I feel so bad for all of you."

"Yeah, it got about as ugly as it can get. We're all still dealing with it. I think it will work out eventually. At least I hope it will."

"Me too. They're such a great couple. They always have been."

"Looks like you and Emma are quite the couple, now," Mike said, elbowing Eddie in the shoulder as they strolled along. "Guess that went pretty well."

"Yeah, thanks to you. She's really great. I still can hardly believe it."

"I'm happy for you Ghetti. You deserve that. It makes me feel good to watch you guys together. A girl like that is so much better for you than that stupid game. You're not still--"

"It's over, Mike. I took it all the way, but now it's completely finished. Do you want to hear about it?" Eddie set his tacklebox down at his usual spot. He stole a quick glance at the pickup location, both relieved and disappointed to see nothing there.

Mike stopped in the middle of setting up his rod. "I don't know, Ghetti. Do I want to hear?"

"I promise it will blow your mind. And you're probably the only person I can talk to about it."

"OK, bring it on."

"Before I tell ya, do you have any idea who the Gamemaster was?"

Mike shook his head. "I got nothing."

"Old Lady Lauffer!"

"No shit!" Mike stood mesmerized, looking like he didn't really believe it.

"Oh yeah. And that's just the beginning. But before I tell you the rest, you gotta promise not to tell anyone."

"Of course, dude. I won't tell a soul."

Eddie retold the adventure of breaking into the Lauffer's garage for the last task, and how Olivia had surprised the hell out of him.

"So, she's like a crazy sick programmer?" Mike still didn't look convinced. "She even had us steal her own damn mermaid!"

"That's right! All part of her plan. And she could hear us through the Hoodlum laptop, so she knew about the trail cam I planted to catch her."

"But why did she make us tear the crap out of the golf course?"

Eddie hesitated. He knew this would be his best chance to come clean with Mike about his role in exposing his father's affair, but part of him still hoped that he might get away without ever confessing at all.

"OK, this is going to sound whacked. You gotta listen to the whole thing. And I'm gonna tell you about something that may piss you off, but I hope we can get past it and still be friends."

"Is it about my father?"

Eddie nodded. It looked like neither of them would do any fishing before he told the whole story.

"I guess I need to hear it. We'll always be friends, Ghetti."

Eddie took a deep breath and began.

"Olivia Lauffer is my grandmother. She was not allowed to talk to me, so the whole game thing was just a way for her to finally meet me. My mother agreed to live next door so I would be near my grandparents, but they were never supposed to talk to me at all."

The expression on Mike's face looked as shocked as his own must have appeared the day before.

"The Lauffer's son was a computer genius, and they planned for him to be a huge success. Like Bill Gates big. They already owned a kick-ass electrical business."

"And their son was your father?"

"Yep. And I'll kill you if you ever tell anyone, but my mother used to work at the Dolly. That's where she was working when she met my dad."

"I promise I'll never tell. Ghetti, you must have flipped. Did you know any of this before she told you?"

"I kinda found out about her working at the Dolly during one of the tasks. But I never put the whole thing together."

"So, what happened to your father?"

"The Lauffer's couldn't deal with their son hooking up with a stripper. They hired some guy to expose my mother as a gold digger or con artist. He broke into her trailer, smashed her in the face with a gun, and my father got shot trying to protect her."

"Jesus, Ghetti. That's unbelievable! This all happened in Sutter Valley?"

"Mostly. I guess some happened in Kendall's Corners. My mother went back to Georgia, where she was from. But the Lauffers had her tracked down when they realized she was pregnant with their grandson. She finally agreed to move back here, but came up with the no contact deal."

Mike looked stunned, still in disbelief. For Eddie, it felt great to share the strange tale and watch someone else react the way he had. Telling the story aloud made the whole thing start to feel real.

"But what about my dad? And the golf course?"

"Olivia just found out she has only a year to live. That's why she came up with the Hoodlum game, so she could meet me before she died. But she also wanted to get back at a few people, too. Before my father met my mother, his parents wanted to fix him up with the daughter of the rich founder of the club. But she was a snob and blew him off. Olivia was still pissed about it, almost twenty years later, so she exposed the girl having an affair. With your father. I'm so sorry, Mike."

Mike turned away. Eddie couldn't tell if he was furious, or about to cry. When he turned back around, he spoke through clenched teeth.

"How did she do it? How did Old Lady...your grandmother know about all this? I heard she had videos of them together!"

"She has the security contract for the club and who knows how many other homes and businesses around here. I guess she has access to pretty much anything she wants."

"And you helped her do this?"

"I did, and I am so goddamn sorry. But I had no idea what it was. The task was to sneak a thumb drive on your father's computer. I swear I thought it was more proof that Geoff had trashed the course. I never would have done it if I had known what it was. I hope you know that, Mike. You guys are like family to us."

Mike stood looking at him for a long moment.

"I believe you, Ghetti. And like my dad said, the affair is one hundred percent his fault and no one else's."

"So, we're still friends?"

"I told you Ghetti. We'll always be friends." Mike picked up his rod and started towards his usual fishing spot on the point.

Eddie could feel a tightness around his chest slowly relax, as though he had just unloaded a tremendous burden. He took a moment to soak in the beautiful fall colors that had overtaken his fishing hole. Until now, he hadn't really noticed.

Mike wound up to cast his line and turned back to Eddie.

"But your grandma's a real *bitch*!"

## Chapter 14 - And the Real Gamemaster is…?

Tina's car sat in the driveway when he biked home after school. She usually went out with her friends on Friday. Even if she didn't, she *never* made it home before five-thirty. What was going on? He dropped his bike and backpack and sprinted inside.

He found her sipping coffee and reading one of her paperbacks at the kitchen table.

"Mom? You OK?"

"Hey Eddie," she answered, giving him a quick peck. "I'm good. Did you think I got fired?"

"I saw the car was home. I didn't know what--"

"Internet is down. They sent us home early. I remembered you had off tonight, so I figured I could spend some time with my favorite guy. That is, unless you have plans with your other woman," Tina smirked.

"No, she's working tonight."

"So, I got you all to myself. Whataya say we go out for Chinese?"

"Sounds good to me!"

Tina tossed him the keys and let him drive to the Chinese restaurant. Though the place wasn't crowded, Eddie chose an isolated booth in the corner. They both had their favorite meals memorized by number and ordered before they even sat down.

"Eddie," Tina began. "We really need to talk. I hope you can someday understand why I didn't tell you about all this."

"Mom, I understand already. I'm not mad at you at all. You've been a great mom, and I don't care what you did when you were young. I know how hard you work to take care of me, and I'll always be proud of you."

Tina's eyes welled up. She reached across the table and held his wrist. "Thank you for saying that, Hon. I hope you know how much I love you."

"I do, Mom. And I get why you didn't want me to spend time with them or live in their house. She really doesn't care much about other people. Just money. And the family name."

"I'm so proud of you; of the young man that you turned out to be. And you did it without much help, too."

"Thanks Mom. But you might not be so proud of me if you knew about some of the things I did for the Hoodlum game."

"Try me, babe. I heard about some of the shenanigans already. How did she get you to do all those things?"

Eddie told her about finding the Hoodlum game with Mike and described the strange rules. Tina listened while sipping her Mai Tai, hanging on every word. She laughed when he told her about painting the sign and stealing the Lauffers' mermaid.

He knew she wouldn't have found these activities so funny before today. She would have lectured him about steering clear of anything that could "ruin his chances of getting into a good college." Now that her own colorful past had been shared, he supposed she would be a bit less judgmental of his behavior. It felt pretty cool to tell her about his adventures over the past couple of weeks. She seemed to regard him as more of an adult.

"That was you guys?" Tina asked after he confessed to tearing up the golf course with the stolen tractor. Again, she seemed more impressed than angry. He didn't share the part about framing Geoff, though. He did feel a little guilty about that, and realized that maybe he was more like the Lauffers than he thought.

She sympathized with Mike getting cold feet after the golf course challenge. She also understood Eddie's need to keep going, however, driven by the desire for cash and the need to unravel the Hoodlum mystery. And soon after that, the video blackmail threat by the Gamemaster trapped him in the game for good. Tina closed her eyes, fully grasping Eddie's predicament.

Despite Mike's forgiveness, Eddie still felt terrible about the Ashland task. He knew this challenge shared none of the humor and excitement of the mermaid or tractor tasks. His mother would feel as much shame as he did. But just like his talk with Mike, he hoped that confessing to his mother would help to put the matter behind him.

As Tina listened, he told her about loading the file from the Hoodlum thumb drive onto Andrew's PC; hating himself for every moment of it. Naturally, his mother had heard about the scandalous presentation. She and Eddie had previously discussed the whole ugly mess, and what might happen to their closest friends as a result. At the time, however, she knew nothing about Eddie's involvement. He fully expected her to criticize him for this one. And he deserved it.

When he finished, he fidgeted with his fortune cookie. He could feel his mother looking at him, as if deciding what she should say.

"Let me ask you something, Eddie. I know you worried about how these secret missions affected other people's lives. You even called Olivia on it. You exposed her as being selfish for not giving a damn for unintended consequences, right? But even though you couldn't have known what would happen, you still feel pretty bad about how things turned out, don't you?"

Eddie looked at her, confused. "Of course I do, Mom. What if they get divorced and move away, all because of me? If I had just done what Mike said, I could have quit the game and none of this would have happened. And Mr. Blackmoore wouldn't be going to jail, and they wouldn't be getting divorced, either."

"But then you wouldn't have learned about your past, right? You might never have discovered your connection to the Lauffers, or realized that one day you will inherit a great deal of money. Does that change how you feel about playing the game?"

Eddie hadn't thought about that. So much in his life had changed over just the last two days. He still hadn't processed the whole thing.

"I am glad I found out. But I still feel bad about the other stuff."

"Well, part of being a grownup is understanding that there are always tradeoffs. Sometimes you have to accept the fact that some bad things happen along with the good. Even when you have the best of intentions, innocent people can get hurt. Do you understand that?"

"Yeah, I guess so."

"So the difference, Eddie, is that you really *do* care about what happens to people. Even when it's not your fault. People like Olivia Lauffer and her late husband most certainly do *not* care. They go out of their way to make really bad things happen to people that they think wronged them in any way. And without a care in the world for whoever else gets steamrolled in the process. And in my book, that simple act of caring makes all the difference in the world."

Eddie considered that for a moment, fiddling with the wrapper on his fortune cookie. "But to the people whose lives I messed up, it won't make any difference to them if I felt guilty about what I did, or that I didn't do it on purpose. The fact is that I did it, and they have to deal with the fallout. In a way, that's almost worse."

Tina raised her head to catch Eddies eyes and cupped his fortune-cookie hand in both of hers. She didn't squeeze too hard, but it was enough to crush the delicate little cookie.

"Eddie, I really think you are being too tough on yourself. Like Olivia said, these people are responsible for a great deal of what happened to them. The killing, the affairs -- they own a big part of their own fate."

"Yeah, but not their kids, though."

"That's my point about the Lauffers. Even this insane game thing she set up. What if you had gotten caught by the police? Or shot while breaking into the Blackmoore's house, or the Dolly? That could've easily happened!"

Eddie looked around to make sure no one could overhear them. Tina picked up on the cue but continued in a slightly quieter voice.

"What would Olivia have done then? Sure, she didn't plan for you, her only grandson, to get hurt or arrested or killed, but what if any of those things had happened?"

Eddie looked up from the pulverized fortune cookie, still sealed in its cheap little wrapper, and shrugged.

"I'll tell you exactly what she'd say," Tina continued. "You heard her say it. 'It's a tough world,' right?"

Eddie nodded.

"That's the battle cry of someone that doesn't give a damn about anyone but themselves. And I'm so proud that you aren't like them, Eddie. You're so much better and kinder than them."

"Maybe," he conceded. "But I still kept doing the tasks for more money. Even after I found out about what had happened to the Ashlands."

"She offered you a crazy amount of money to do these things. She knew damn well that for someone in our financial situation, you really had no choice. Just like me at the Dolly. And she was blackmailing you and your friend with proof of your involvement in the other crimes."

"Jesus, Mom. With that kind of logic, I could just as well be a drug dealer. Or a hit man!"

"You know what I mean. She took unfair advantage of our limited finances to get you to do her own bidding. She's a master manipulator of this whole town and has been for a long time."

Eddie nodded again. He opened his mangled fortune cookie and dumped the remains on his plate. He didn't want the cookie itself, but they always read their fortunes. It was part of their ritual.

"Eddie, I know you've been through a lot these past few days. But there's something else you need to know."

"What is it?" Based on the look on his mother's face, Eddie could tell this was going to be another shocker.

"What if I told you that someone else had out-played the master manipulator. Someone else had beaten her at her own game. What would you think of that?"

"I-I don't know." Eddie stammered. "What do you mean? Who was it? My father?"

"No, Baby. It wasn't your father. It was me." Tina looked at Eddie tearfully.

"I don't get it. What did you do?" Eddie asked. Before he had a chance to read it, his printed fortune slipped through his grasp into a puddle of kung pao sauce on his plate.

"I'm so sorry to put you through even more of this, Eddie. I didn't realize how much it meant to you to know about your father. But I understand now, and I really want you to know. No more secrets."

Eddie stared at her wide-eyed, now more confused than ever.

"Karl Lauffer wasn't your father. I was already pregnant when I met him, and I just couldn't find the right way to tell him.

He was so good to me, and I really did love him. I promise you that I wasn't after his money, like his mother claimed. And I was going to tell him about you the same night that bastard cop came in and killed him. And then it didn't matter. I told the cop I was pregnant just to save myself from being shot, and he told the Lauffers about my baby."

"So they just figured I was Karl's."

"Yes, and I thought that would be the end of it. Blackmoore's threats scared me enough to go back to Georgia, but I was too ashamed to move back in with my father. Then less than a month after you were born, the Lauffers contacted me with their proposal. It hadn't even occurred to me that they considered you their own flesh and blood. I realized that I finally had the power to make a big move, so I did. I mostly wanted to punish them for killing Karl. And I was afraid if I let them get too close to you, they'd think up some way to take you away from me forever. I came up with the 'no contact' deal, and they agreed. It was all based on a lie, but it got us our house and got me a job, and someday maybe it'll get you a huge inheritance. But I swear to you Eddie, I never planned it like this on purpose."

"You really did beat the Gamemaster at her own game. Even though you didn't really mean to."

"That's right. And I'm so sorry, Eddie. For that one, you were the unintended victim in all of this."

Eddie shrugged, his head still spinning from yet another wrinkle in this week of revelations. "So who the hell is my real father?"

"I'm ashamed to tell you, but he was the manager at the Hello Dolly. I didn't love him, and he treated me like crap. But I was scared and living on my own in a strange town. He did protect me from the other jerks that frequented the place, but that's about the nicest thing I can say for him. He never knew about you. I didn't keep in touch with him, but I do know that he was killed in a bar fight in New Orleans about eight years ago. They put it in our local paper, since he used to live here. I saved the clipping for you at home, just in case this day ever came."

Tina drew a deep breath and waited for Eddie's reaction.

Eddie didn't react at all. He reached over to finally read his fortune, hoping for anything to lighten the mood. The pool of sauce had rendered the tiny strip of paper illegible.

"So as far as Olivia knows, I'm still her grandson. And you're the only one who knows about my real father."

"That's right, Eddie. You could tell Olivia the truth about your real father, or you could play this out as a Lauffer and stand to inherit a fortune. I know I just hit you with another bombshell, but I promise I will stand behind you, whichever path you choose. Now it's your turn to be the Gamemaster."

Eddie dropped his smeared fortune back into the sauce and stared out the window.

David R. Stookey

# Thank You!

Thank you for reading *The Hoodlum Game*; I hope you enjoyed it! If so, I would greatly appreciate your review on Amazon.

## Amazon Author Website

https://amazon.com/author/davidstookey

## Facebook Author Website

https://www.facebook.com/profile.php?id=61560922540865

## Other titles by David R. Stookey

*A Curse Eternal – The Tragic Account of the Flying Dutchman*

## Short Stories

*Bad at Math*

*The Helpful Neighbor*

*The Last Survivor*

*Dead Man's Shoes*

*Punch and Parry*

www.ingramcontent.com/pod-product-compliance
Lightning Source LLC
Chambersburg PA
CBHW050015180626
46810CB00002B/421